THE SPACE WARP

In Annex 10 in the Adirondack Mountains in New York, the scientists under the leadership of astronomer Dr. Gray can hardly believe the things their instruments are telling them; but, because their equipment is absolutely reliable, they *have* to believe, and on that ill-fated June 30th, they begin to see the chaos will affect mankind.

The Earth is growing steadily hotter. Temperatures rocket as the sun shines through the night and the world is plunged into endless day. Everywhere people are suffering—rich and poor, criminal and family man—and none know if or when relief will ever come. Is this the end of the world as we know it?

Borgo Press Books by JOHN RUSSELL FEARN

1,000-Year Voyage: A Science Fiction Novel
The Crimson Rambler: A Crime Novel
Don't Touch Me: A Crime Novel
The Empty Coffins: A Mystery of Horror
The Fourth Door: A Mystery Novel
From Afar: A Science Fiction Mystery
The G-Bomb: A Science Fiction Novel
Here and Now: A Science Fiction Novel
Into the Unknown: A Science Fiction Tale
The Man Who Was Not: A Crime Novel
One Way Out: A Crime Novel (with Philip Harbottle)
Shattering Glass: A Crime Novel
Slaves of Ijax: A Science Fiction Novel
The Space Warp: A Science Fiction Novel
What Happened to Hammond? A Scientific Mystery

THE
SPACE WARP

A SCIENCE FICTION NOVEL

JOHN RUSSELL FEARN

Edited by Philip Harbottle

THE BORGO PRESS

MMXII

THE SPACE WARP

FIRST BORGO PRESS EDITION

Published by Wildside Press LLC

www.wildsidebooks.com

DEDICATION

For Claire Jane King

CONTENTS

CHAPTER ONE
THE FAULT IN SPACE

For a single star suddenly to blaze from tenth to first magnitude in a matter of hours is by no means uncommon, and when it happened on the night of June 9th, no astronomer thought very much of the occurrence. Just routine. BZ/94 had probably become a nova, was recorded as such on the star-plates and spectroheliographs, and that was that.

But on the next night it happened again—and this time as many as three stars were involved. Unusual, yes, but nothing to become alarmed about. Once again astronomers faithfully logged the occurrence and continued with routine observations, the guardians of the world against the unexpected from space, unsung heroes as important to the safety of Earth as once had been the lighthouse keeper to shipping.

Dr. Gray, chief astronomer of the Mount Wilson Observatory in California, was one of the many scientists who had witnessed this strange flaring up of stars in the vast depths of space, and he had had an unique view of the happening with the great reflector with which the observatory was equipped. Certainly he did not expect that June 11th would again see strange behaviour amongst the stars—but it happened!

He was in the midst of calculations essential to his profession, and the electric clock on the polished wall indicated three a.m. when an excited junior astronomer tapped hastily and entered the doyen's retreat. He came hurrying over to the chief's desk with manifest urgency. "Dr. Gray, if you can spare a moment? I just can't make head or tail of what's happening."

"Happening?" Gray looked up in surprise.

"Tremendous increase in the brightness of the stars, sir. You know it happened last night, and the night before that, but *this* time—!" and the assistant stopped half in awe

With a frown Gray rose hurriedly to his feet and preceded the younger man into the main observatory. All the lights were dimmed to a mere glow and a solitary spot cast upon the small writing desk beside the eyepiece of the mammoth instrument. Dr. Gray seated himself and then controlled the gasp of surprise that almost escaped him. Straight ahead of him, in the reflector's circular field, were Sagittarius, Hercules, and the myriad hosts of the constellations, and every star was of a brilliance that stung the eye.

Gray reached out and snapped a switch. Immediately a blue-tinted shield slid into the high-magnification eyepiece and this in itself was the first hint of the unusual. Never in astronomical history had the stars been so brilliant that they could not be studied with the unprotected eye.

Antares, Cepheus, Hercules—all of them flaming and scintillating with a brilliance never before seen by man.

Nor was it a wavering brightness but an intense and steady glare. The remoter constellations, riding far out into the Milky Way, were gleaming in supreme splendour. In fact the whole area within a peculiar V-shaped wedge was alive with uncanny brightness.

"Extraordinary," Dr. Gray muttered, and the remark covered his emotions completely. He was too experienced a man to show how startled he really was. Pondering, he rose from the reflector-seat and wandered to the outer door of the dome, the assistant astronomer padding softly behind him. They stepped together onto the balcony surrounding the dome and gazed at the portion of the sky towards which the telescope was trained.

There was no doubt about it. Something was wrong up there! In the clear Californian air, rendered even clearer at this height on the mountain range, the stars in one particular area were infinitely more brilliant even than Sirius, occupying a different quarter of the heavens. It was as though sheer void existed up in that one section, and air—with its masking effect—everywhere else. Which, of course, was an impossibility.

"What do you make of it, sir?" the assistant asked, his voice tense.

Dr. Gray did not answer immediately. He looked down towards sleeping Los Angeles, then out into the remoter darkness where lay the night. Then once more he glanced towards the sky. Hands in his pockets he walked slowly back into the observatory and the assistant closed the door behind them.

"I never saw anything quite like this," Gray admitted at length, switching on the main lights to reveal his grimly puzzled features. "Of course, stars do blaze up mysteriously sometimes, surging rapidly from tenth to first magnitude and then dying down again—but that all the stars in one section of the sky should behave that way is astounding! Even the constellations and nebulae are not immune."

The assistant waited for more words of wisdom, but none came. Abruptly making up his mind, Dr. Gray hurried from the main observatory into the radio-television department. In a few minutes he had established contact with other observatories throughout the darkened hemisphere of Earth and notes were exchanged.

Not only on that night did Mount Wilson link up with Greenwich and the major observatories of every country, but for several nights afterwards. Finally the entire mass of information was sifted and pooled and a conference took place behind closed doors in an unnamed city.

"There seems to me to be no doubt about it, gentlemen," Dr. Gray said seriously. "Earth is speeding at a million miles a minute towards an area of uncanny brightness. But what this brightness is we don't know."

"Correction," responded the expert from Greenwich. "I have here the conclusions of Marsden and Yates, two of the best astrophysicists in the world. Their contention is that the increase in light is caused by a fault in *space itself*! Ahead of us space is not behaving as it should. The old-time scientists used to refer to the ether of space, which they considered to be the only way in which we can explain the medium that carries light and heat vibration. A kind of universal sea in which all radiations move. Now we believe that the propagation of light-waves and other radiation is simply a property of space-time itself. In the past, small flaws in this over-all sea of space have apparently caused stars to flare up brilliantly, to die away again to normal afterwards when the flaw has corrected itself. We can none of us explain the sudden appearance of brilliant stars—but the theory of Marsden and Yates suggests that the actual fabric of space-time itself, like any other material medium, is liable to discontinuity. It can develop a warp, and from the look of things it has. A huge, terrifying warp, towards which Earth is flying nearer with every second."

"Have—have the consequences of this phenomenon been fully weighed?" Gray asked presently.

The Greenwich astronomer gave, a grim nod. "In a matter of two weeks or so Earth will inevitably touch the outer edge of this fault in space and will then speed on into the core of the disturbance. What will happen we do not know yet, but in the two weeks left to us we can probably find out."

"Governments must be informed immediately," declared the representative from France.

"I disagree," interposed Sweden. "I, at least, must have tangible evidence before I dare stampede my Government with this kind of thing. Science is so little understood by the masses. One word in the wrong place can start a panic."

So the astronomers wrangled and argued, but they finally closed the meeting with the decision to work out every possibility as near as they could and then submit their findings to a conference of selected delegates from every country in the world—and this was exactly what they did.

The meeting took place ten days later, in secret. No television cameras whirred, no newspaper man was admitted. Here was a matter of the utmost solemnity affecting not a portion of the human race, but all of it. As on the earlier occasion Dr. Gray was chairman, and he explained the situation in detail.

"And how long will it be before we reach this—this figurative flaw in the fabric of space?" questioned the American delegate.

"We have four days," Gray answered quietly.

"Do you believe it will mean the end of the world?" asked Russia in surprise, and he was answered by his own astronomical expert.

"Not necessarily. It is not a matter of colliding with a solid body or being swung aside by some superior gravity. It is a matter of—er—conditions. The end of the world, as such, is unlikely, but the effect of this space-warp region on human beings is unpredictable."

"We have no comparison by which to measure," Gray explained. "It has never happened before and all our tests can show us is that heat and light will no longer obey natural law until the warp has been spanned."

"And how long will that take?" asked Australia.

"We don't know. There is such tremendous depth in the cosmos we just cannot accurately measure how far the flaw in space extends. Summing up the issue, gentlemen, Earth will swim into this mystery region at approximately three o'clock in the afternoon of June thirtieth, four days hence. All of you here, representing your respective Governments, must take the warning to the leaders and they, in turn, in the most palatable manner they can devise, must break the news to their peoples."

"That is not difficult," China commented, "but in return the people will ask for preventative measures. What are we to tell them to do?"

"I think that can be summed up in three words—'Stay at home'. People must be urged not to travel unless they really must, and panic movements must be prevented at all costs. As for actual protection against this approaching mystery we have nothing to offer because we just don't know what we're getting into!"

* * * * * * *

So, quite unashamed of its ignorance, astronomy handed the matter over to Government. In consequence, that same night, the first hint of unexpected things to come went out over the airwaves in every conceivable tongue. In Britain the warning supplanted the normal news bulletins and tens of millions of viewers and listeners looked in. surprise towards their sets as the announcer spoke: "Attention, everyone! Attention, everywhere!"

Then a pause. The very method of giving the warning was arresting. No news bulletin, even at the start of the last war, had ever been prefaced like this. The announcer paused dramatically, then continued: "This message is transmitted as a warning, and you are asked to listen to it in all seriousness and, should you know of somebody who has not heard it, kindly repeat it to him or them. The Press will cover the details tomorrow and warnings will go out repeatedly at fifteen-minute intervals henceforth. A message from the Government states that it has been advised by the astronomical faction of the world, representing every country, that there lies ahead of us a cosmic disturbance. The nature of the disturbance is not fully known, but it is believed to be connected with the fabric of space itself, the all-surrounding medium in which our planet moves.

"At approximately three in the afternoon of June thirtieth, four days hence, our planet will swim into this mystery area in the natural course of following its orbit. When that happens it is possible that heat and light waves—and all other radiations that include radio waves—will undergo drastic changes and no longer conform to scientific law as we know it. The effect of this is unpredictable so, until the disturbance has passed—its exact duration is not known—you are advised not to travel. Stay put! For precaution extinguish naked light. Lay in food supplies. Do not travel! Do not travel!"

Some people understood what the announcer was talking about: the vast majority did not, and when an average man does not understand a thing he ignores it and continues to make his plans as before. Samuel Baines and his family, for instance. They had made up their minds to spend their summer holidays in Derbyshire—which was to include an exploration of the Great Peak Cavern—and no warnings about 'staying put' were going to stop it. In fact many holidaymakers, whose holidays coincided with the date of the supposed strange happenings, made no alteration in their plans—not from obstinacy but just because they did not understand.

In England generally the balance seemed to lie between those who were entirely indifferent and those who were secretly scared. Martin Horsley, for instance, a wealthy man and a confirmed invalid, made plans to leave immediately for a small hotel in the heart of Sussex. He had been there before—a lonely old-world place miles from anywhere. For some reason Martin Horsley had the mistaken idea that if he hid himself he would be safe.

Far and wide the warning reached, transmitted by the radio and television stations of every country. One of those hearing it was Woodstock J. Holmes, eminent American financier on vacation in Florida, and his first thought was how he could buy himself out.

The ships at sea, the aircraft, those in outlying places of the world: every one of them was, if possible, warned of the approaching calamity and each reacted according to his or her nature.

Despite the endless repetitions of the warnings and the gathering sense of urgency that crept upon everybody as the days passed by, there were four people who did not give a hang about the stars being bright. On June 30th, towards ten in the morning, they drove out of London in a black saloon, and each one of them had the appearance of belonging to some high niche of society.

The two young women lounging in the back of the car were

exquisitely dressed in the height of summer fashion—one blonde and the other brunette. The two men in front were also immaculate in lounge suits. The man who was not driving had his head bent as he read the morning paper intently: the other had his cold blue eyes fixed on the busy traffic ahead of him.

The two women talked occasionally to each other—the blonde in a hard-bitten style and the other in quieter tones, even with a touch of shyness.

Briefly, the two men were killers—products of London's vast underworld, their outward immaculacy only achieved on stolen money. Neither man was conscience-stricken by his record or murder: quite the contrary. Mike Woodcroft, at the wheel, had the face of a tiger, and hard blue eyes, whilst "Prayerbook" Meigan, seated next to him; was much more subtle. He was the psalm-singing slayer, preferring the slow destruction of the mind by taunts and pinpricks rather than the out-and-out cold-blooded killing.

The women? Women are women the world over, be they the pick-ups of ruthless criminals or the quiet wives of city clerks. They usually possess the redeeming virtue of a streak of gentleness in their make-up, even if it is cat-like. To this latter class belonged Evelyn Woodcroft, the blonde. She had been Mike's right hand during the days when he had started his career of crime. At first her conscience had bothered her, then because there was no cure for this ailment as long as she belonged to Mike—who, in spite of everything, she loved deeply—she had sought refuge behind a brazen exterior and had on three occasions committed murder rather than look sentimental in Mike's eyes.

Janet Meigan was different—very different. She was too good to be mixed up with this bunch. She had married "Prayerbook" under the impression that he was a man of the church: and now she knew the truth she could think of no way out of her predicament, which would not involve the finding of her dead body in the river. Against two men and a woman, all of them killers, she knew, and so did they, that she stood no chance.

At the moment they were heading out of town to spend the day at Woodcroft's hideout in the country—a small bungalow which he had bought against the day when he might have to dive for cover. That day had come. Behind the quartet in the heart of London a financier and his wife lay dead. From Mike's point of view it had been a very necessary elimination. He had "attended" to the man and Evelyn to the woman. Later, by night, they would all hop on a plane for Europe and then....

"Know anything about science?" asked Prayerbook after a while, slanting a placid grey eye towards Mike.

"No. And I don't wanter."

"Pity. I know a bit. Paper's full this morning about this thing what's supposed to happen to us."

"Oh, that!" Mike spat with scorn through the open window:

"Maybe something in it. It says here that space has gone cockeyed and that because of that it's difficult to explain what's going to happen."

"Then why bother anyway?" Evelyn enquired, crossing her shapely legs and lighting a cigarette.

"I'm not botherin' exactly," Prayerbook retorted. "It's these fellers in the paper I'm talkin' about. Listen to this an' brush up on your science: Normally, light waves are transmitted through space in the form of waves, and anything from violet to red, between the ranges of three thousand and seven thousand Angstrom units is visible to us. The other vibrations are not, being in the invisible spectrum. But, if as seems likely, a fault has developed in the medium we call space it is possible that the two vibrations of which we are most conscious, light and heat, may take on different properties. Either may change their rate of vibration; new and unknown wavelengths may reach us. The breakdown of an apparently immutable law makes it impossible to predict what may happen. Earth is hurtling straight towards such a flaw in space now and towards mid-afternoon today unusual effects may be noticed. People should be on their guard and—"

"Aw, shut up!" Woodcroft interrupted, with a sideways

glance. "What the hell do you want to be reading that bunk for? Haven't we enough on our minds as it is? Concentrate on the moment! We've tough work ahead of us, Prayerbook. Rubbing out Crocker and his wife means we've got to get out of the country quick as we can."

"I know, I know," Prayerbook grumbled, slapping the paper down on his knee. "Can't blame a feller for doing a bit of thinking, though."

"But surely there can't really be anything in this scientific stuff?" Janet Meigan asked, her brown exes reflecting a vague disquiet. "With the TV and radio warnings and now these glaring headlines it makes you wonder—"

"Bunk!" Woodcroft decided, setting his square jaw. "Just something to fill the paper. The scientists have been pretty quiet lately since the talk about a World Atomic Pact. They have to do something to boost circulation!"

Woodcroft's remark stopped all conversation concerning the flaw—for the time being anyhow. And whilst it had been proceeding an omnipotent observer would have beheld Earth sweeping onwards in her orbit, nearer and nearer to that mystery region where lay the unknown.

And in faraway Florida, Woodstock J. Holmes, the great financier, was becoming somewhat concerned for his eighteen stones of blubber. Warnings had been battering at him, and everybody else, for such a long time he was commencing to take notice. Suppose there was something in it? And, because he possessed so much money and influence, even to owning the main airline between Florida, New York, and London, he was able to pay the expense of a famous American scientist to come and talk things over with him in his hotel.

"What I want to know, Sheldon, is: how will it affect me?" Holmes strode up and down the fan-cooled room as he talked, motioning with his fragrant cigar. "I'm too big a man to be involved in some scientific hocus-pocus which might upset my financial plans."

Sheldon, as cold-blooded a scientist as any alive, eyed the

tycoon steadily. "Big man or otherwise, sir, I'm afraid it means trouble," he answered. "As for your financial interests—their continuation depends on how things work out."

"Everything is as vague as that?"

"I'm afraid so."

"What kind of scientists do you call yourselves? Before stampeding the world as you are doing you should work out some kind of preventative measure. You fellows live too much in the clouds. You forget how many interests are going to be disturbed by this—this something."

"We have no preventative to offer, Mr. Holmes, and warning had to be given." Sheldon hesitated, looking puzzled. "Might I ask why you sent for me? Surely not just to repeat what has already been broadcast?"

Holmes came to a stop in his pacing, his jowls shaking as he thumped the table beside him. "I want you to tell me where I can find sanctuary. Where is the best place to go? The Tropics, the Arctic, or what? Which spot on this planet is the safest?"

"There will not be one. The Eskimo and the Hottentot will be equally affected. Don't you understand, Mr. Holmes, that we just don't know what will happen? But we do know that the entire Earth will be involved."

Holmes gave a grim smile. "Now you listen to me, Sheldon! Science, the treasured baby of the Government these days, must have made some kind of preparation for this potential disaster— or whatever it is. Science loves its secrets far too much to leave them open to possible destruction. You and other scientists must have some spot on this Earth where you feel you can perhaps be safe. Where is that place? I have the right to know. Dammit, my own money founded the Institute of Molecular Research, anyway! Not that I know a thing about molecules, but my accountants tell me I might as well be philanthropic."

"All scientific formulae and other things of value have been transferred to Annex 10 in the Adirondack Mountains," Sheldon answered. "Annex 10, in case you are not aware of it, is a full-sized building built as a retreat in case of war. It is overshadowed by a gigantic mountain ledge that protects it from the air, and it stands at least five hundred feet above ground level. Every scientist of importance is also there, waiting to study this space-warp phenomenon when it arrives."

"That's all I wanted to know." Holmes stubbed his cigar out in the ashtray. "I'm coming back with you. I'm as important as any scientist—in fact more so. Without my money science would be in a mess anyway."

"I shall have to get permission," Sheldon said, reaching for the phone—but Holmes stopped him.

"Permission be damned! That I shall be with you will be enough. We'll leave right away."

In face of which there was, nothing Sheldon could do, but he wondered how his brother scientists would take it when the money-bags strode into their midst.

* * * * * * *

Meanwhile, in England, Martin Horsley had arrived at his old-world hotel in the heart of Sussex. It lay well back from the main road, screened by elm trees. The nearest habitation was five miles away, hence the hotel was useful only to those who owned their own cars. It was exclusive, hush-hush, and possessed a proprietor-manager highly skilled in the art of handling wealthy clients.

Grumbling and grousing, as pale as death and about as substantial, Martin Horsley alighted from his Rolls limousine and tugged a plaid blanket irritably about his bony shoulders. "Took you long enough to get here!" he reprimanded the poker-faced chauffeur. "I'm about frozen!"

"Sorry, sir," the chauffeur apologised, and wondered how any man could be frozen in midsummer.

"You will be, Dawson—you will be! I don't forget things like this. Bah! Nobody cares a hang how much I suffer."

"No, sir."

"Eh?" Horsley aimed beady eyes and the chauffeur coughed.

"I mean yessir. Sorry, sir."

"Fetch the luggage and stop muttering."

The chauffeur obeyed, but he went on muttering—under his breath. Stumping his heavy stick on the gravel of the driveway Horsley advanced to the hotel, passed under its ancient archway, and so into the main hall where the proprietor was washing his hands with invisible soap.

"Delighted to see you again, Mr. Horsley. Delighted! How are you?"

"Rotten—and stop blabbering. What rooms did you reserve for me?"

"Same as before, Mr. Horsley. I think you—"

"They won't do. There are bats in this place and I can hear them at night. Change the rooms."

"But, sir, I—"

"Change 'em!" Horsley nearly shouted, and the proprietor fled behind his reception desk to make hasty alterations in his allocations. Finally he smiled.

"I have just the right place, Mr. Horsley, if you'll come with me. You'll like it. Overlooking the countryside. As you say, most of the upper rooms do carry the sound of bats at night. They're in the old disused belfry on the top of this building. It used to be a church, you know."

"I didn't know and I don't care. Show me the room."

Still growling and grumbling Horsley crept up the stairs and into the room the proprietor indicated. No man—not even Horsley—in his right senses could have found fault with its clean freshness and country-aired linen.

"Not bad," he grunted. "And what provisions have you made for this nonsense which is supposed to happen later his afternoon?"

"Provision?" The proprietor looked vague.

"From the look on your face, man, I begin to wonder if you know what I'm talking about!"

"Oh, yes, sir, I know. This strange business in space. The newspapers are calling it an 'ether-warp'. Most unusual, I suppose. Certainly I haven't made any particular provision. I don't see how one can. I don't even know what ether is."

"I do. I've had it numberless times with these blasted operations of mine. So you've made no preparation. Not much use me coming here, was it? I came specially to get away from this ether-thing."

"I'm sure you'll be as safe here as anywhere, sir," the proprietor said, hopefully if not convincingly.

"I'd better be. Otherwise I'll hold you responsible! And where's Dawson with the luggage?"

"Right here, sir," the chauffeur answered, coming in with the first consignment.

* * * * * *

At about this time in the depths of the African jungle Henry Brand, an illegal trader in protected animal species, was turning a possible cosmic disaster to his own unscrupulous uses. At the moment he was seated in his bungalow, his base of operations, with his black head boy at the other side of the crude table. And M'Bonga was looking startled, the whites of his eyes dilated against the shiny coal-black of his skin.

"I don't believe you can't get near the animals," M'Bonga," Brand said deliberately, pointing a finger at him.

"It's true, bwana. This strange weather is affecting them. They hide from us—"

"If you and those lazy devils out there don't start getting results, I'm going to use white man's magic and do things to the sunlight that will make your ears drop off!"

"Bwana do—do things to—that?" asked M'Bonga, glancing through the crude glassless window towards the hot stillness of the forest, the sun glinting occasionally amidst the foliage.

"Correct," Brand agreed solemnly, and swallowed some whiskey. "You and the rest of those boys have been too lazy lately. It's over a week since you've brought me any animals, and my buyers are getting impatient. If you don't start getting results I'll frighten the lives out of you."

M'Bonga hesitated, not quite sure what to make of the situation. He was fairly educated and, within limits, loyal, but he had within him the profoundly superstitious fear of his ancestors and the thought of the white man doing something to the lord of day genuinely frightened him. Then he remembered something and half turned as he was about to leave the bungalow.

"Bwana blot out sun?" he asked, with strong memories of a solar eclipse he had witnessed.

"No, my friend. I'll make it three, four, twenty times brighter, and shrivel your souls to Hades!"

M'Bonga bolted, genuinely scared, to get some action out of his boys. Brand grinned and glanced towards the silent radio. He was much too obtuse to realise that the radio warnings were serious, yet, surprisingly enough, he had spoken a great truth to M'Bonga when he had said what he would do to the sun.

CHAPTER TWO
WORLD ON A GRIDDLE

Between Macclesfield and Leek a somewhat ancient tourer was snorting its way. Samuel Baines sat at the wheel, his round face wreathed in a satisfied smile, a Panama hat of doubtful age pushed onto the back of his greying head. Beside him, likewise smiling, sat his wife Claire. All the noise came from the rear of the tourer where Bertie and Gwen were doing their best to out-shout each other. And, on the ancient rack at the back, was strapped the luggage. In a word, Samuel Baines, insurance clerk, had made up his mind to take his holiday with the family as arranged. As yet it was only ten-thirty in the morning. By mid-afternoon they would be domiciled in the rooms they had booked in Derby; afterwards they could—and would—roam at will. As for the radio warning they had forgotten all about it. It was a perfect summer day with a fleece or two of cloud here and there and a soft southerly breeze. Stay put indeed!

Then the argument of the two children at the back brought the matter into focus again. It gradually dawned on Samuel Baines what they were talking about.

"I tell you it isn't the same ether you get stuck on your face!" Bertie insisted.

"I say it is!" Gwen retorted. "Can't be two sorts of ether. Doesn't make sense. My schoolteacher says that—"

"Bertie's right, Gwen," Samuel Baines cut in. "There's the ether you use for making people unconscious, and the ether our world is floating in."

Silence for a moment, except for the convulsive efforts of the car. Baines hoped no more questions would be asked because he was not sanguine of his scientific ability to answer them.

"How do you know our world floats in it?" Gwen asked suspiciously.

"Well—er—I don't really; but scientists say it is so."

"And if something goes wrong with it everything else goes wrong, too?" Gwen persisted.

"Not everything else," her father answered, doing his best to think fast. "Just those things that rely on ether for their—their power of transmission. For instance, if a liner sails from England to New York, it does so by using the ocean as the medium on which to sail. But a storm at sea can agitate the ocean so much that the liner may miss its destination entirely, even turn completely around, or generally behave in a manner it wouldn't in the ordinary way."

Samuel Baines blew out his cheeks and wondered how he had ever managed to think thus far.

"Then in this case," his wife said, who had hidden depths of understanding which often surprised him, "things which use ether to float on may do as the liner would at sea, eh?"

"That's it!" Samuel Baines agreed. "Light and heat are the main things which travel on ether. So if something goes wrong with the ether for awhile, something will also go wrong with every sort of radiation which travels on it!"

"Which makes me right," Bertie decided.

"Right!" his sister hooted, swinging on him. "Why, that's what I said!"

"It wasn't!"

"Was!"

And with the vision of another endless juvenile argument looming Samuel Baines sighed to himself and drove on steadily through the hot sunlight.

* * * * * * *

Also in the sunlight, but many miles from Samuel Baines and his family, was Douglas Taylor, the radio-engineer. The firm of radio manufacturers by whom he was employed were more or less compelled to obey the Government's injunction to 'stay put', and though it meant telling every employee to go home, it was perhaps the safest. If anything happened to anybody it would not be the responsibility of the firm. So, at a loose end after having reported for work in the usual way, Douglas Taylor gravitated, as he usually did, towards his Nissen hut where he spent his spare hours experimenting with the possibility of receiving radio communication from an extra-terrestrial source. That there were professional scientists engaged on the same work in America and other countries, all using vastly superior apparatus, did not faze him in the least. It was simply something that he enjoyed, a hobby verging on an obsession.

The hut stood in a field off the main road leading into the Peak District, a field raised high above the others and barren of any pasture. Fortunately the owner was a kindly, rusticated farmer who did not in the least object to the young man's 'crazy' hobby even though he did secretly wonder at the bristling festoons of wires and complex dish-like aerials, which sprouted from the hut's roof.

Douglas Taylor stayed long enough to collect some lunch and a thermos flask full of tea at his rooms, and then he set off. He reached his hut around noon and, to his surprise, had hardly entered it before he was joined by his friend and fellow enthusiast, Gordon Briggs. Briggs followed the occupation of motor mechanic, but his heart was in science and his lively imagination was fired by the thought of possible communication with an alien civilization.

"Never expected to see you, Gordon," Douglas smiled, holding out his cigarette packet. "Did the garage pack it up?"

"Uh-huh. The boss got the idea that since we've such a lot of inflammable stuff about the place we'd better shut and go home. I had a hunch you might have been told to do the same thing, so here I am. No effort for me to detour to here since the garage is only about a mile away down the road."

Douglas nodded, lit his cigarette, then rid himself of his haversack. Gordon looked about him upon the familiar array of gadgets and radio apparatus, and finally towards the powerful generator which took its power from a main overhead feed-line, by special permission of the Electricity Authority. Finally he asked a question: "Do you think there's anything in this warning business, Doug? You're a better scientist than I am."

"It's my belief the warning is perfectly genuine," Douglas answered seriously. "Something is due to happen to this old world of ours which never happened before—or if it did we have no record of it. Come to think of it, some of the Biblical references might be meant to record such a happening. However, be that as it may, I have the uncomfortable feeling we are not going to enjoy ourselves after four o'clock this afternoon."

Gordon was silent for a moment, tall, pale-faced, red-haired. Usually he smiled his way through life but this time he looked almost melancholy. He glanced through the window of the hut onto the perfect summer morning outside. "Hard to believe anything can change that!" he exclaimed.

Douglas only half smiled to himself. Ever since being a boy he had, from the sheer love of it, spent his time studying scientific books, beginning with an old volume that had belonged to his grandfather, *Eddington's New Pathways in Science*, and because of that he knew just how much relies on the continuity of the fabric of space-time. His conception came close to reeling when he tried to imagine what might happen with that essential medium disturbed. As the scientists had said, the results would certainly be unpredictable. It was beyond human ingenuity to forecast just what would happen.

"Come to think of it," Gordon said, sitting on an old office chair, "aren't we rather wasting our time trying to pick up radio signals from space, in view of what's going to happen? If space itself goes cockeyed what hope have we of trying to establish a contact? We've failed even when space is normal, so we certainly won't succeed when it's cockeyed!"

"That," Doug said deliberately, "is the point, old man. Because we don't know how space will react I'm pinning my hopes on the fact that its very craziness may give us a chance. The agitation in it may even make us able to bridge the gulf, where normally we can't. As to wasting our time—well, is there anything else we can do? The only alternative is to sit down and bite our nails while something happens, and that certainly won't do for me!"

"Okay, I asked for that. I'm wondering, though, if the solar systems around other stars will be as much involved in this spatial disturbance as ours will be?"

"It seems logical to assume so. The astronomers don't seem to know the full extent of the flaw so it's hard to say how far-reaching it will be."

"Suppose—" Gordon hesitated over the thought in his mind. "Suppose it proves to be infinite in extent? I mean, what if Earth goes swirling onwards into an ever-widening flaw that has no end? What will happen to us?"

Douglas turned his thumbs down significantly and then settled in front of the radio receiver, and made sure that the recording apparatus was operational.

"Without wishing to seem too much of a wet blanket," Gordon apologised, "something else occurs to me. Surely the powerhouse engineers will cut off all electricity as four o'clock draws near? They've been warned to extinguish naked light as a precaution—if one can call electricity a 'naked light'."

"One can as far as radiators, electric arcs, and such like are concerned." Douglas frowned to himself for a moment. "I hadn't thought of that, and it will certainly kill our generator if the power stops. On the other hand they may think it necessary to keep power flowing for many reasons and rely on individuals to guard against naked flame."

Gordon ran a hand through his red hair. "Sounds silly to me. Where's the point in extinguishing a naked light. What good will that do?"

"Kind of precaution. With space having gone queer there is

no telling how heat may be transmitted or what it might do. Anyway, as far as the powerhouses are concerned we shall have to trust to luck."

* * * * * *

Also viewing the immediate future with concern was Commander James Rilson, captain of the *Queen Enid*, the largest Atlantic sea-going liner afloat. In common with all other ships at sea instructions had been received to proceed immediately to the nearest port, but in the case of the *Queen Enid* this could not be done because she was equidistant from Britain and New York, right in the centre of the high seas.

Rilson called his officers to a conference in his cabin and regarded them seriously. "Just what is going to happen, gentlemen, we don't know," he said, his craggy face betraying the responsibility he was shouldering. "Our course is such that we cannot possibly reach either Southampton or New York before four o'clock this afternoon, so all we can do is go straight on. At the moment we are four hundred miles north of the Azores and we must maintain schedule. I have radioed back for instructions and been informed that we stay on course. However, should anything of an exceptional nature occur it is up to us to calm the many passengers we have on board. That understood?"

The officers nodded silently, each one filled with the dire feeling that they were up against something they did not understand.

"We are seamen, not scientists," the Commander finished, "and we shall be true to our code as near as we can. The one thing we must prevent at all costs is panic, so I look to you to prevent it if it shows any sign of developing."

More than this he did not say because, like everybody else, he had no idea what was coming. So the conference broke up and the various officers returned to their posts, each vaguely wondering how things would work out since all the passengers had themselves heard the warnings over the radio loudspeaker.

Two of the many hundreds who had heard them were on the promenade deck at the moment, gazing out over the lonely summer sea. It seemed as though on this particular day, the one that threatened to find Nature going completely crazy, the weather was doing its utmost to provide compensation. Even the great liner's movement through the ocean produced hardly any breeze at this particular portion of the deck.

"Do you think this 'something' that is supposed to happen will be anything like the end of the world, Den?" the girl asked, gazing out to sea.

She was slender, dark-headed, her eyes full of vague speculations as she looked up from the ocean to the unblemished blue sky.

"I don't know." The young man beside her, Dennis Archer, put a protective arm about her slim shoulders for a moment. "I don't see how it could be. One doesn't talk of the end of the world as one would a coming shower. The end of the world is such a gigantic thing the mind just doesn't register it. No," he decided, after thinking for a moment, "I don't believe anything like that is foreshadowed. There would have been far grimmer warnings if that had been in prospect."

"Then do you think it might go dark?" It was plain the girl was searching for something onto which she could anchor her mind. "If something is destined to go wrong with light-waves I suppose everything could stop being visible, couldn't it? I mean, the only reason why we see things is because of the light reflecting from them."

"True," Dennis admitted; then he forced a laugh. "I never thought my beautiful young wife was so scientific!"

"The beautiful young wife isn't," Betty smiled, glancing at him. "I'm just repeating what I once learned as a schoolgirl."

Dennis did not answer. They could neither of them escape the conviction that their conversation had a hollow ring. Their minds were centred on only one thing—four o'clock, and what would happen then. Everything else, even the fact that they were only just married and that a trip to New York was their honeymoon, just would not register. Up there, beyond the blue of the sky, beyond the warm blaze of sunlight, something incomprehensible was looming—and coming ever closer.

* * * * * * *

It was about this time that Mike Woodcroft, his wife, and two companions had stopped at a roadhouse for lunch. They soon got on the move again, though they felt they were safe enough from the police because of a screen of alibis and legal preclusions. Just the same, murder had been done and the sooner they made their first dive to cover in Woodcroft's bungalow, the safer they would feel.

They reached it about half-past-three. It was a perfect hideout, built entirely of wood and completely isolated, the driveway being concealed by dense trees. Few cars ever travelled the deserted road that led to it.

The two women were the first to enter the long living room with its wooden furniture, skin rugs, and small private bar let into the wall. Evelyn Woodcroft glanced around to assure herself that all was in order, then she pulled off her light dust-coat and tossed it on one side, began to fluff her blonde curls with the tips of her fingers.

"Gosh, but it's hot!" she exclaimed suddenly, and went across to the window to fling it open. She was not aware of it, of course, but she had uttered the first intimation of a change in the supposedly immutable laws of physics.

That it was hot there was no denying. Usually, in England; even in the midst of summer, there is nothing approaching the tropics in temperature, but this afternoon the air had become completely motionless, the sun blazing down in unclouded splendour, heat oozing out of the wooden walls of the bungalow, out of the floor, and out of the roof.

Evelyn went across to the wall by the fireplace, pressed a button, then watched the wooden shutter covering the bar go sliding back. Reaching down behind the small counter she dragged out Scotch and a full soda siphon. Glasses clinked. By the time Janet had taken off her coat, and Woodcroft and Prayerbook had come panting into the room, Evelyn had four drinks ready. Without saying a word to each other they drank— and then drank again.

"Maybe I got the idea wrong," Prayerbook said meditatively, cocking a grey eye towards the sunshine through the open doorway, "but I had the impression we came here to cool off before startin' for the airfield tonight. Cool off! It's hot enough to fry eggs on the floor!"

"What d'you expect me to do about it?" Woodcroft asked sourly.

"Take a look at this thermometer!" Janet exclaimed, studying it where it hung on the wall. "A hundred degrees! And unless I'm crazy it's still rising!"

Janet Meigan was not crazy. Not only that particular thermometer but every thermometer in the world was expanding its mercury. An inexorable climb in heat had commenced. Heat radiations, relying on space for their transmission and normalcy were the first to undergo the effect of change. Or at least they appeared to be the first. It was Mike Woodcraft's suggestion that they break the monotony until evening by watching the television that brought a surprise. Evelyn switched it on and, though the power was there as usual, nothing came forth. Impatiently she fiddled with the controls, trying different channels. There was only silence.

"Damned thing's gone dead!" Mike decided; glaring at it.

"I wonder—" Prayerbook glanced at it and put down his empty glass.

"What d'you mean, you wonder?" Mike thumped the top of the set violently. "Obvious, isn't it?"

"I'm just remembering something, going right back to when I was a school-kid. I was pretty keen on science then. Television and radio waves, if space went haywire, would perhaps be the first to be affected, especially the long ones. Working slowly up the scale, we'll find Hertzian waves, dark heat waves, infrared, light waves, and all the rest of them being affected in turn as the wavelengths grow shorter. Cosmic rays would come last, the shortest of all."

Nobody spoke because none quite knew what Prayerbook was talking about, or what was implied. But the scientists did, the world over, and their faces grew grimmer as they studied their instruments and received reports. Soon the radio waves died out and every lonely scientific outpost was left to grapple with the problem alone.

In Annex 10 in the Adirondack Mountains in New York the scientists under the leadership of astronomer Dr. Gray could hardly believe the things the instruments told them, but, because the equipment was absolutely reliable they had to believe, and with the unfolding seconds from four o'clock on that ill-fated June 30th, they began to see what chaos was in store for mankind.

Amongst the scientists stood Woodstock J. Holmes, the financier. He was neither welcome nor necessary, but as he had expected his power and influence had shoe-horned him into this secret retreat of science and now he stood watching the experts at work, quite unable to understand what they were doing or the nature of their conversation. A lot of jumping needles on immaculate white dials meant nothing to Woodstock J. Money was his only concern in life, and just at this moment he was very much afraid that he was doomed to lose most of it.

"What the devil are you fellows monkeying about for?" he demanded at length. "Can't you say something? Explain what is going to happen?"

"It is already happening," Dr. Gray answered, without looking up from his calculations.

"Happening? What is? I don't see anything different!" The financier strode across to the big window and, gazed out onto the mountainside. Heat-mist below hid the view there, but else-where everything seemed peaceful enough—except that the Annex was surprisingly warm considering it was shielded overhead by a gigantic out-jutting lip of rock.

"At four o'clock precisely Earth flew into the outer edge of the space flaw," Gray continued, rising to his feet. "The first signs of aberrant space became immediately obvious in the swift decline of radio communication. Long waves went first and now the short ones have gone too. Next in the spectrum line come the heat-waves, and those are being affected at this very moment. Surely you've noticed how hot it is in here?"

"Yes." Holmes looked about him. "Why should it be?"

"It's because of an abnormal state of the fabric of space—what used to be called the ether. Naturally, heat waves are transmitted through space at the rate of four hundred-billion to the second: any variation can make the temperature rise or fall prodigiously. In this instance it has risen—and may possibly go on rising to tremendous heights! Normally our aqueous atmosphere intercepts four-tenths of the full heat of the sun, but even that isn't operating properly. And there's another side to this heat business—"

Dr. Gray stopped and considered, mopping his face.

"Well?" Holmes barked at him. "What?"

"The tests we have just been making reveal that the heat waves are passing through solids as easily as light-waves pass through glass! That's why it's so hot in here. The rock-covering over our roof is of no use at all. We might as well be exposed to the naked glare of the sun."

"Must be something wrong with your instruments," Holmes declared at length. "Even I know that something solid will block heat, and it doesn't have to be so very solid, either. What about those big umbrellas, like they use on the beach in Florida? They—"

"This," Dr. Gray interrupted, trying to be patient, "is an abnormality. No umbrella, not even rock, can prevent heat waves blasting through at the moment. Look at the thermometer there."

The financier did so and whistled. It registered 118 degrees Fahrenheit, and was still rising. Then his gaze snapped back to the troubled scientist.

"How long does this frying process go on?"

"As yet it is impossible to forecast because we don't know the area of the fault in space."

"Dammit, don't you scientists know anything?" Woodstock J. roared. "Every question I ask you hedge round. We're just getting no place."

"If, as we assume, the ether waves are to be progressively disturbed to the limit of the spectrum we can expect light itself to be affected next, and light covers a multitude of wavelengths. It means that red, orange, yellow, green, blue, indigo and violet will all be affected. It may still remain light, but it will be of an order to which we are not accustomed. Later still will come the ultraviolet radiations, then the X-rays. And so on through gamma into cosmic. Everything that relies on ether for transmission will be changed."

The financier tugged open his already unfastened shirt collar and mopped his face. Perspiration was trickling down it so copiously he had ceased to attempt drying it.

"How do you suppose this business is affecting the outer world?" he asked finally.

"We can only guess." Dr. Gray had returned to his instruments. "Since radio has failed we have no exact idea, but I should imagine the first consequence must be fires of far-reaching extent."

"But it can't be this blasted hot everywhere, surely? What about the Arctic and Antarctic?"

"Since the sunlight and heat-waves are penetrating solids at the moment there must be a temperature rise at the poles also," Gray answered. "Even on the night side of Earth, and the south pole where at this time of year night lasts six months, the heat of the sun must be driving straight through Earth. I should imagine there must be chaos in the polar regions with millions of tons of ice and snow on the move."

The financier pulled at his pendulous underlip. "Must be somewhere where it's cool," he muttered.

"Not on this planet," Gray answered quietly, and at that Holmes swung round and came striding over to the scientist as he sat amongst his colleagues before the instruments.

"Look here, Dr. Gray, I don't like your calmly fatalistic attitude! You accept this whole unnatural business as though it were an everyday occurrence. You, and the rest of these so-called experts around you, ought to be up and doing and trying to find means to put things right."

Dr. Gray smiled wryly. "Do you imagine we haven't tried? Do you imagine we can pattern the infinite when we haven't even the vaguest idea what has really happened to space?"

"Then you ought to have! What's the use of science if it lets us down in a dilemma?"

"We can only work from known premises, sir," commented the acid-faced Sheldon.

Holmes banged his fleshy fist on the bench beside him. "Great heavens, if I ran the money markets like this there would be utter chaos! I always did think scientists were dreamers and fools, and now I'm sure of it. But I don't think any one of you is such a fool as to refuse a fortune. I'll pay any sum—any sum, mind you—to the man who transports me to a place where it's cool and comfortable until all this hocus-pocus with the ether is finished."

Nobody answered, but one or two of the scientists gave bitter smiles. The unspoken suggestion that he was being humoured like a naughty child stung Holmes to further words.

"Don't tell me that scientists don't want money as much as anybody else! Or is it that you mooned around with your theories so long you don't remember what money is?"

Dr. Gray got to his feet, a tired look on his features. "Mr. Holmes, you came here uninvited because you believed your money entitled you to do so. Very well. I have tried to tolerate your presence, but I am finding it increasingly difficult. Will you kindly realise that money, as such, may not have the slightest value if this ether tragedy continues. The whole world may go up in flames, and your money with it. Even if there were a cool, comfortable spot on this planet—which there isn't—do you suppose any one of us recording this business and trying to think of ways to stop it, would take time out to make one man comfortable? Hardly! What you want now, Mr. Holmes, is faith in your Maker, not your bank account."

The financier glowered. "Who do you think you are talking to? I am the President of—"

"Yes, yes, I know," Gray gestured wearily. "Have the goodness to leave us alone, Mr. Holmes. There are rest rooms in the adjoining section of the Annex. Maybe you'll find it cooler there."

Holmes hesitated, genuinely unable to believe that for once his financial power and eminence had let him down. He took a glance at the thermometer, saw that the mercury had climbed three more degrees on the scale, and then he strode angrily to the adjoining door.

CHAPTER THREE
WORLD IN TORMENT

Martin Horsley, sprawled full-length in the deep armchair of the bedroom in his Sussex hotel, was slowly becoming aware that something was different somewhere. Since his thoughts were always centred on his own condition it could only mean that the difference lay in his body. Then he realised what it was: he was warm for the first rime in many years. Thus he lay for a while in the dreamy peace of his discovery, his sleepy eyes peering outside onto the sun-drenched elm trees. Not a leaf moved. Whether there were sounds outside or not he did not know because the windows were tightly shut to preclude all possibility of a draught.

It was probably ten minutes after Horsley had discovered that he felt comfortable when there was a hesitant tapping on the door.

"Come in," he murmured, and through screwed-up eyes saw Dawson enter. He looked uncomfortably warm in his dark chauffeur's uniform and was carrying .a medicine bottle and tumbler upon a tray.

"Well, what do you want?" Horsley demanded. "Can't you see I'm dozing?"

"Yessir—sorry, sir. But you did tell me to remind you when it was time for your medicine, and it's time now. Half-past four."

"Medicine? Medicine! What would I want with that beastly stuff? Dr. Carslake wants shooting for ever prescribing such muck."

Dawson opened his mouth and then closed it again. For hypochondriac Horsley to be talking like this was absolutely incredible.

"Matter of fact," Horsley said, struggling out of his chair and straightening up, "the one thing I need at the moment is the best meal this hotel can produce. Tell the proprietor I say so."

"Meal, sir?" Dawson stared stupidly.

"You're not deaf, are you?" Horsley demanded, flinging aside the plaid shawl from his scrawny shoulders.

"No, sir, of course not, but as a rule you only eat the lightest of foods specially peptonised and everything—"

"Confound it, man, don't stand there arguing! Do as you're told!" Then as the baffled Dawson turned towards the door Horsley went on talking. "Y'know; Dawson, it's a funny thing, but I never felt quite like this before. I feel comfortable, almost contented."

"Yes, sir," Dawson answered vaguely.

"It sort of crept upon me," Horsley mused. "As I sat there in that armchair. It began by my feeling warm. I felt as if the thousand and one ills by which I am beset were commencing to loosen up. They haven't gone, mind you! Lord, no! I have a great deal to lose yet, but somehow—"

"Possibly the warm afternoon, sir," Dawson suggested. "The thermometer in the hall downstairs was over a hundred when I passed it a few minutes ago. That's very high for England—"

"Did you say it is about half past four?" Horsley interrupted, frowning over a thought.

"Twenty-five to five now, sir, to be exact."

"I was just thinking about that disturbance which was going to affect us around four o'clock. It must have been about that time when I began to feel so much better."

"Far as I can see, sir, no disturbance has happened. It's warm, of course, but you expect it in June."

"There's more than warmth in the air, Dawson." Horsley had started pacing up and down the room, grasping at the air with one claw-like hand as though he expected to catch hold of something. "You can't feel it, perhaps, but I can. I don't quite know what it is but by heaven I like it! Anyway, tell the proprietor that I want the best meal he can provide at six o'clock exactly. If he raises objections send him to me and I'll buy the confounded hotel!"

"Yes, sir," mumbled the still dumbfounded Dawson as he went on his way. Something incredible had happened to his irate employer, and he had not the vaguest idea what.

And, in a different way, Henry Brand—the illegal animal trader in the African jungle—was also being affected by the change that had come upon the world, though like most other people he was hardly aware at first that a change had come. It did occur to him that even for the African forest the temperature was dizzyingly high, but nothing more than this at first came to his notice.

His earlier demand for the capture of animals had still not been met, and Henry Brand was not the type of man to be satisfied with vague excuses about animals behaving strangely, much less so when he had been drinking heavily and when the heat was as terrific as at the moment.

Putting down his drained whiskey glass he lurched unsteadily to the bungalow door and then stood there panting, his gross, powerful body stripped to the waist, rivulets coursing down his broad chest. For a moment or two, as well as the fogs of drink would permit him, he watched the natives supposedly at work in the nearby clearing and two things dawned on him in quick succession. One was that they were working with obvious languor, the heat being beyond anything even they were accustomed to; and the other was that with the moments they were becoming less visible by reason of gradually obscuring vines and twining undergrowth: It was the first time Henry Brand had ever seen vegetation grow as he looked at it. He did not know whether it was an hallucination or whether he was more drunk than usual. In any case he meant to find out.

Reaching to the wall beside the doorway he took down a leather-thonged whip and then strode down the bungalow steps.

Out here, thick though the foliage was, the heat was like the interior of an oven. Brand did his best to ignore it and strode across to the clearing where the natives were working on assembling nets and traps—then they swung round as Brand's voice bawled at them.

"What the hell are you lazing about for? Get on with your job and get out there. It's hot—sure, but what else do you expect?"

"Bwana, it is too hot for work," his head boy, M'Bonga, protested. "And the animals are in hiding."

"Don't try that excuse on me, M'Bonga: I know you too well! Lazy! The whole wretched lot of you! Remember what I told you would happen if you didn't get any animals?"

The native nodded uneasily, his eyes on the whip in Brand's hand.

"Well I meant it!" Brand spat. "I said I'd make the sun so hot it would shrivel your hides to blazes. That's what I'm doing now! Can't you feel it blasting the very life out of you?"

M'Bonga nodded fearfully and with a grim smile Brand looked on the startled natives to the rear—then he frowned and looked at his feet. Something was wrong somewhere for, despite the density of the forest which usually completely screened the sun, he could see his own shadow cut on the swelling, surging vines that crept about his feet. He glanced upwards in amazement and saw the sun shining with pitiless brilliance—shining through the foliage. It didn't make sense. Yet there it was and, in glancing upwards—even though only for a moment—Brand felt as though white hot irons had passed through his eyes He howled with sudden pain and went stumbling away to his bungalow to seek more whiskey and, perhaps, the chance to drown out the fantastic things that seemed to be happening to him. Being practically on the equator, and at a point on Earth more directly in a line with the sun than anywhere else, he was becoming involved in scientific changes that had yet to spread to the rest of a sweltering world.

Not that it was sweltering in the Great Peak Cavern of Derbyshire whither Samuel Baines and his family had gone to spend the first afternoon of their holiday. At the moment they were following the main rugged pathway, which led into the limestone depths—and, to their satisfaction, there were no other 'explorers' in sight at the moment.

"I've heard of bigger places," Samuel Baines commented, pausing to look about him upon the six great chambers branching from the entrance track. "One day maybe we'll see them."

"Not on your salary, dear," his wife commented, smiling sadly. "Anyway, what other caves are there? I'm not very well up in geography. Or is it geology?"

"You should read more, Claire," Samuel Baines told her. "There's the 'star chamber' in the Mammoth Cave of Kentucky, for instance; and then there's the Margaret River Caves in Western Australia; there's the Wookcy Hole Cave; the Blue Grotto of Capri—"

"Yes, dear," Claire agreed, "but at the moment we're in the Great Peak Cavern of Derbyshire, so what do we do?"

"Explore!" Samuel Baines held his walking stick aloft. "What else? Come on!"

The four of them began moving, the sound of their feet on the loose stones echoing back to them from confining walls. Remotely—so much so they were not sure if they really heard them—came the sound of voices and other footsteps as visitors like themselves explored distant portions of this massive earthwork.

"Whatever we do," Samuel Baines said presently, when they had come some distance from the main entrance, "we must keep together and follow these recognised tracks, and we must obey the signs—"

He pointed to them. They were brief and to the point. One said *This Way Only.* Another said *Danger—Keep Clear.* Yet another, upon which young Bertie set his eyes with mischievous intent, said *Unexplored Track—Keep Away.*

"If we go straight on," Samuel Baines continued, taking his wife's arm, "we can't come to any harm."

"But, dad, I thought you said we were going to explore!"

Gwen grumbled. "Where's the use of exploring if you don't come to any harm?"

"I'll bet Captain Scott wasn't afraid of coming to harm," Bertie objected.

Samuel Baines paused and then turned deliberately. "Captain Scott and ourselves are not to be mentioned in the same breath," he said. "We're just tourists looking round a cave. Captain Scott was an explorer."

"But, Dad, I thought you said that was what we were!" Gwen exclaimed.

Samuel Baines looked at his progeny for a moment and closed his eyes momentarily; then with an air of resolution he swung back and began walking again, Claire dutifully at his side.

"Not as cold in here as I'd thought it would be," Claire remarked at length, picking her way among the stones.

"From all accounts the temperature maintains a level of about fifty degrees Fahrenheit," her husband answered. "Inside here we're protected from external temperature variations—so be it snowing or blazing outside we still remain at about fifty degrees."

"But, Sam, it isn't fifty: it's seventy."

"Can't be," Samuel Baines said flatly.

"Then the thermometer we just passed must be a liar. It registered seventy, which seemed to me a pretty high figure for the interior of a cave."

"Oh, well...." Samuel Baines wrestled with the enigma silently for awhile as he walked along. "Maybe a warm draught of air blowing in from somewhere. Notice how cleverly they have carried lighting into this place?" he asked, changing the subject quickly.

Claire surveyed the overhead cables, which had been swung onto stapled insulators in the rockery. The lamps glowed with an intense brightness in the dustless atmosphere of this sanctuary. "Wonder how they climbed up there to put the cables?" she hazarded.

"Scaffolding," Samuel Baines replied knowledgeably. "And

it looks to me as though we're coming to an end of this track. Wonder where we're supposed to go next?"

He paused and glanced behind him, intending to consult Bertie and Gwen. Not that he gave a hoot for their opinions anyway but as part of the family they had to be considered. Only Bertie and Gwen were not in sight. There was only the stone path overhung by the dancing globes, leading back to the entrance to the cave.

"Where—where are they?" Claire asked abruptly, as she grasped the situation.

Samuel Baines' brows knitted. "Wandered off, I suppose, and I distinctly told them to stay with us!"

"I don't remember you saying so, dear."

"Well, if I didn't they should have known that anyway! We'd better look."

His walking stick firmly grasped in his hand Samuel Baines began to retrace—at first slowly, expecting to see the youngsters any moment; then he travelled with increasing urgency when he failed to find them. Finally he stopped, his harassed wife by his side. "Bertie!" he shouted. "Bertie! Gwen!"

The rolling echoes flung his voice back at him, but there was no answer from the missing children. Claire caught at her husband's arm. "Sam, what do we do? Where are they? Should we try and get the police, or a search party, or something?"

"Nonsense! We'll find 'em."

Though he was anything but hopeful of doing so Samuel Baines strode forward again, until presently he and his wife reached the fenced-off right-angled pathway, which said *Unexplored Track—Keep Away.* In the dust and loose stones at the base of the fence were distinct small shoe-marks.

"Gwen's!" Claire exclaimed. "Look! You can see the mark of her rubber heels. Sam, they've followed the track over the fence! The very thing they shouldn't do!"

Her husband smiled in relief. "Nothing to worry over, Claire. They wouldn't be normal kids if they didn't go poking around where they shouldn't. Soon find 'em. Think you can climb over this fence, or won't the rheumatics let you?"

"Neither rheumatics nor anything else'll stop me finding my children!" Claire retorted, and grasped the wooden uprights of the barrier to prove her statement.

Even so it took her some five minutes, with Samuel's help, to scramble over the fence and drop heavily on the other side. Here she stood breathing hard in semi-gloom until her husband dropped beside her.

"The little idiots!" he muttered. "No lighting is carried along here and it'll be as black as the tomb further on. Why can't they do as they're told. I'll skin 'em alive when I find 'em."

"You brought a torch, didn't you?" Claire asked.

"Uh-huh. Give me time to find it, can't you?"

Claire ignored the tension under which her husband was labouring. There were convulsive movements in the gloom as he tugged the cheap torch from his jacket-pocket. Then, he switched on the thin beam and waved it ahead of him along a downward-sloping rocky trail, which led into apparent extinction. "What possessed them to explore along here, and in the dark?" Samuel Baines demanded, advancing slowly. "The pair of them must be crazy."

"Gwen had a fountain-pen torch on her blazer," Claire said. "I gave it her for her birthday, remember? Not that it provides much light for a spot like this."

Samuel Baines' only response was a grunt. The trail, being followed was extremely narrow and, presently, it became only a thin lip on the edge of a sheer wall of rock. To the other side loomed emptiness, some mighty volcanic chasm blown in the earth in the unguessable past and into which Baines' torch beam failed to penetrate.

"Lord!" he whispered, pausing. "Surely they didn't—?"

He looked into the abyss and then at his wife. There was a second's deathly silence—then Samuel Baines yelled with all the power of his lungs: *"Bertie! Gwen!"*

It seemed an interminable time before the echoes died away— and hardly had they done so before they were followed by an answering cry. It sounded as if it came from another world.

"Here! Down here!" It was the plaintive but unmistakable voice of Bertie. "Give us a hand, Dad. We can't get back."

"The little idiots!" Samuel Baines breathed wrathfully, quite spiteful now he knew they were still living. "What the blazes are they doing down there?"

"What on earth does that matter?" Claire demanded. "The thing is to locate them and get them back safely. Whew, but it's hot in here!" She broke off, tugging off her heavy tweed coat.

"Yes, unusually so." Samuel Baines looked about him with some mystification in the torchlight. "Shouldn't be hot in this underworld. Anyway, that doesn't matter. Here, hold the torch and I'll see what I can do."

He removed his jacket and then lay flat on his face and peered into the gulf. The weakness of the torch was infuriating. All he could see was darkness.

"Hey!" he shouted. "How did you get down there, kids?"

"It was Gwen's fault!" Bertie shouted from a distance.

"Wasn't, Dad! It was Bertie's!"

"Never mind whose fault it was" Samuel Baines yelled. "How did you get down? How far below are you?"

"We fell down," Bertie answered out of the gulf. "I think Gwen's sprained her ankle. We're about—two hundred feet down. With fingers and toes you can do it."

"You hope," Baines muttered, and debated whether or not to go for a search party. Claire settled it for him.

"How much longer are you going to play around, Sam? Hurry up!"

It was obvious Claire was far more concerned for her children than her husband—and Samuel Baines knew it. He muttered something to himself and then slid himself over the rocky ledge and began to feel his way down. "Nice damned way to spend a holiday this is!" came his mumbling protest. "I'll skin 'em alive when I get to 'em."

"Yes, dear, but hurry up!"

Her husband looked upwards for a moment and saw a dim

vision of his wife's head and shoulders behind the brightly haloed eye of the torch—then there was a sudden gasp from her and the torch disappeared. There was a clink in infinity and then utter, crushing darkness.

"What the hell!" Samuel Baines screamed.

"I—I dropped the torch." Claire's voice above sounded disembodied. "It's—down there somewhere."

Samuel Baines clung on desperately, more frightened now than he had ever been in his life before. Finally he mastered himself far enough to shout again. "Hey, Bertie! Is that torch down there? Can you find it?"

"No, Dad. We're on a ledge and there's a drop we can't see just beyond us. Torch must be down there. Haven't you got matches?"

"Matches! Matches, he says!" Baines breathed hard.

"How the heck do you expect me to get at matches when I'm hanging on here by the skin of my teeth? Anyway, I haven't any. Only a lighter which works when it thinks it will—"

"Go on down, dear," came Claire's urgent voice. "I'll go and find somebody to help us—if I can see my way."

Baines heard her scrambling movements amidst the stones above and he cursed the cramp in his fingers. Gently he began to edge himself downwards—until the inevitable happened. His brittle fingers refused to grip any more on the rockery and his hold slipped. Down he went, to crash with such force that the senses were knocked out of him.

* * * * * * *

And, not more than a dozen miles from the Great Peak Cavern, Douglas Taylor and his red-haired friend, Gordon Briggs, sat before Douglas' complicated radio equipment. The time was 4:30 and all radio communication had disquietingly died out some time ago. Both young men sat in their shirtsleeves but even so perspiration was pouring down their faces and the little Nissen hut had a temperature as high as a bakehouse.

"I still think this is crazy," Gordon said, lighting a cigarette. "With all radio waves completely dead how can we possibly hope to receive anything from out of space?"

"Earth radio waves are dead, sure," Douglas agreed, after a glance at the silent loudspeaker, "but that is possibly because any point on Earth is quite near to us when compared with the multiple light years to other stellar systems. On Earth we're in the very epicentre of the spatial disturbance: we have no guarantee that the disturbance is so absolute in outer space."

"But surely, man, it must be? The entire Solar System has swum into this fault, hasn't it?"

"Uh-huh—but don't get the situation wrong, Gordon." Douglas turned to look at him directly. "Space hasn't disappeared, remember: it has only become altered and agitated by reason of a fault, just as a sheet of water doesn't disappear when a wind passes over it. It merely becomes agitated, but it is still there."

"From which you infer what?"

"Damned if I know, really, but as long as space exists, be it agitated or normal, I'm hoping it might be possible to get some results. In fact I'm hoping it more so because Earth's own radio waves are completely blanked for the time being, which ought to make the way clear."

"Then isn't night a better time with solar static absent?"

"Makes no difference. Solar static is there all the time. Night only happens on a revolving planet. In space the sun is shining all the time, and releasing his electronic disturbances. That isn't any bar at all."

"There's one thing I do know," Gordon said, getting to his feet and moving restlessly. "It's infernally hot in here. I can hardly breathe!" He crossed to the thermometer and looked at it; then he started. "Hundred and twenty-five!" he gasped. "Who the heck ever heard of a temperature like that in Britain?"

"Spatial agitation," Douglas said ambiguously, his lean fingers playing with the controls of the radio equipment. "And I hope they don't cut off the power or we're sunk."

In this respect he had no need of worry. Government orders throughout the world had commanded that power of the electrical variety should stay on since it did not constitute naked flame; and in any case vital needs had to be fulfilled. Most utilities were still working in the insufferable heat, and hospitals too were compelled to maintain power supply. Indeed, by and large, humanity at the moment was only suffering one inconvenience and that was the preposterous mercury climb.

"Wonder what it's like outside?" Gordon Briggs hazarded, and moved to the door of the Nissen hut.

"I shouldn't if I were you!" Douglas exclaimed sharply.

"Eh? Why not? Be cooler."

"On the contrary, you're liable to find it hotter and it is also possible that out in the open there may be radiations getting through from the sun which don't normally reach us. Some in the region of the seventh octave are deadly. They can produce blindness and paralysis. Better stay where you are. This tin roof isn't much protection, I know, but it's better than nothing."

Douglas glanced about him once and then turned back to the radio equipment, adjusting the headphones on his ears. Gordon reflected, then he opened the door, but did not go outside. Instead he stood gazing into an unbelievably bright afternoon, the heat waves dancing on the rugged landscape and the distant hills mysteriously glowing with the intensity of the light-photons striking them. It was quite the most 'sizzling' summer afternoon Gordon had ever seen.

"I get the impression," he said presently, turning back to the hut, "that tin isn't much use against the sun. What do you suppose we could do to stop the heat getting through?"

"Nothing," Douglas answered bluntly.

"Huh?"

"I mean that. I've no proof of it, but I think the heat waves are going clean through the interstices of matter. This heat isn't just the temperature rise you get through radiation of heat waves on a tin roof: it's the actual heat waves, naked and unadorned, boring straight at us."

"In that case, then, whatever other radiations there may be—like the seventh octave ones, for instance—must be boring through too?"

"Probably. Just take our chance—" Douglas stopped dead for a moment and tensed forward, his fingers twisting the control knobs on his radio apparatus.

Gordon bent close to him. "Hear something?" he asked tensely. There was a second or two's pause before Douglas shook his head ruefully.

"I thought I did for a moment. Atmospheric hum, I'm afraid. It could have been a voice, pitched in such a key that it doesn't make sense to us—or maybe I'm imagining...." He gave a sigh. "Reception of any kind of signal is going to be in the lap of the gods. The space warp is going to make it as difficult for radio waves to travel as for a liner to steer a straight course in a tempestuous sea—"

* * * * * * *

Not that the Atlantic Ocean was tempestuous at this moment. It was calmer than a sheet of glass, yet its horizon limits were masked in a pearly haze that had a phenomenal brightness all its own. It was beautiful and yet terrifying at the same time, as though a glowing curtain of swan down were slowly closing in on every hand. And, overhead, the blinding bright sun emitting its torrent of insufferable heat.

Nobody was on the deck of the liner *Queen Enid*, and she was also motionless in the calm sea. Down below in the stokehold and engine rooms the men were unable to work because of the heat. Even the strongest of them could not stand up to a temperature of 153 degrees Fahrenheit, which was the registration in the bowels of the ship. So Commander Rilson had done the only thing possible—ordered a complete halt in activity until there should be a let-up in the weird phenomenon that had struck the world. He himself, and most of the crew, were in their cabins, trying to recover for the brief spells on the bridge which must be kept if the giant vessel were to be safely handled as it lay to.

In the main lounge passengers were sprawled about as though dead, limp with the heat, calling incessantly for drinks that were brought by waiters who could hardly drag one foot before the other.

Dennis Archer and Betty Walford had gone beyond the stage where drinking satisfied them any more. What was the point in constantly drinking when, the moment the liquid had been consumed, thirst rose again to terrifying demands? Right now they lounged half asleep in armchairs, breathing heavily, mopping their streaming faces at intervals.

"I once went through the Persian Gulf," Dennis said at length, speaking with effort, "but it was a blizzard compared with this lot."

Betty stirred languidly. "How long will it go on, do you suppose?"

"No idea. Nobody knows— Oh, steward!" Dennis raised a limp hand and a steward came over to him. "Yes, sir?"

"Any information as to how long this business is going on? Has the Captain issued a bulletin or anything?"

"'Fraid not, sir. Trouble is the radio is out of action and there's no news from anywhere." The steward looked worried. "Never saw anything like this before, sir, and I've been making this trip most of my life. Becalmed—and hotter than anything I've ever known."

"What's our present position?" Dennis asked lazily.

"About four hundred miles north of the Azores, sir."

"Okay. Thanks very much."

"Which means nobody knows what to make of it," Betty said. Then she forced a little laugh. "How right you were when you said it wouldn't go dark! It's just the opposite, judging from the view through the outlook window there."

Dennis frowned. "I don't recollect saying it wouldn't go dark."

"Well then I asked if it would and you didn't answer. Lord!" Betty half staggered to her feet and swayed, "I can't stand much more of this, Den! I've got to have some fresh air. I'm going up on deck."

"Captain Rilson has forbidden it." Dennis made an effort and rose up beside the girl.

"I don't care if he has: I can't stand this. Come on." Whether it was against regulations or not did not concern them at the moment. All they wanted was some kind of respite from the overpowering warmth—for here, right out on the open ocean, there was nothing to prevent the sun's heat rays beating down mercilessly through every portion of the liner.

And it was the same for all ships at sea. Many had made port and disgorged their passengers and crew to places that, whilst still warm, were not so grilling as on the open ocean. But other vessels were like the *Queen Enid*, becalmed and roasting like the inside of an oven.

It was neither better nor worse on deck, as Dennis and Betty discovered. They did not take the risk of going out into the naked sunlight. Instead they remained in the shadow of the liner's superstructure, hoping for a cooling breeze from the haze-swathed ocean—but none came. There was only the motionless air and the burning rays that felt as though they would melt the very bones themselves.

"Becalmed we may be," Dennis said presently, "but I get the impression that we're drifting. We're not at anchor, anyway, and there is a slight movement."

"Does it matter?" Betty asked hopelessly. "Much more of this heat, Den, and we'll die. You know we will. It's more than flesh and blood can stand."

She was right there, and Dennis knew it though he would not admit it. If the thermometer mercury climbed any higher heat prostration would be rife throughout the liner. Every one of the passengers, and possibly the crew as well, would die of blazing heat and torturing thirst.

"Captain Rilson's on the bridge, anyway," Dennis said at length, nodding in the bridge's direction. "He must be as tough as iron to stand it. I've a mind to have a word with him."

"Isn't allowed, Den. The bridge is one spot where—"

"I'm going anyway. Rilson may know something and anything's better than this sizzling uncertainty. You stay here in the shade."

"Not if you go," Betty insisted. "Whatever happens to you might as well happen to me."

Den shrugged and took her arm. Together they advanced from the shadows and into the blaze of the sun. The moment they did so they realised they had to run for it to prevent themselves fainting. Its force on their unshielded heads was like a spear driving into them. They began running and in a few seconds reached the steps leading up to the bridge. Five minutes later they were within the bridge itself, cut off once more from the direct sunlight. Commander Rilson and his first mate, both of them stripped to the waist—and a similarly nude sailor in shorts controlling the wheel—glanced round at the arrival of the pair.

"Passengers are not permitted on the bridge, sir," Rilson said briefly. "Kindly leave this moment!"

"This isn't an ordinary occasion, Captain," Dennis responded. "Surely if we've taken the risk of hurrying through that ghastly sunlight outside you will have the courtesy to answer a few questions?"

"Meaning?" Rilson looked tautly into the pearly distances.

"Put simply, Commander—what's wrong? How did we ever get into this Turkish bath?"

"You knew perfectly well what has happened, sir. The radio warnings were full of it before radio waves unfortunately ceased to operate. We are in the midst of a flaw in the ether of space and the whole world is involved."

Betty sat down heavily on a tip-up stool against the wall. "Haven't you some idea when it will cease, Captain?" she asked. "After all, you have access to information denied to the passengers."

The Commander, his rugged face gleaming as though water had been thrown into it, glanced at her. "Believe me, madam, if I had any way of getting information as to what is likely to happen next I'd pass it on to everybody on this vessel immediately. As it is I just don't know. The only concrete thing seems to be that the temperature is still rising. In the stokehold it registers one hundred and sixty-two. On the open deck it is one hundred and forty-eight."

"It can't go on!" Dennis insisted. "If it does—"

"If it does," Rilson said quietly, "we shall die. There are no two ways about that."

"What would happen if we went for a swim?" Betty asked, after a brief silence. "Would it be—cooling?"

"I would say it would be fatal," Rilson retorted. "If you decide to swim in these conditions, madam, I will take no responsibility for what may happen. Please understand one thing: all known laws are crazy at the moment. Not only heat waves. Our compasses, for instance, are hopelessly wrong. The magnetic attraction of the North Pole is no longer operating as it should. Our needles are swinging aimlessly."

"Then I was right!" Dennis exclaimed. "We are drifting slowly!"

"Correct—but I have no idea where. This haze envelopes everything. It is safer to drift to nowhere in particular than try and steer a course without a compass. We can at least pull ourselves up in case of an impending collision. Near as I can tell by the sextant we're moving in the direction of the Azores—"

"Or somewhere," the first mate interrupted suddenly, looking intently through the window. "Take a look at that, sir. What do you make of it?"

The Commander was not the only one who peered into the distance. Dennis and Betty peered over his shoulders, and the man at the wheel strained up on tiptoe.

"It's Egypt!" Dennis said abruptly. "Look! You can see the Pyramids and the Sphinx. No possible doubt of it."

Commander Rilson blinked, more shaken than he had ever been in his maritime life.

"That's ridiculous," the first mate said bluntly. "We have

drifted a little, certainly, but we're still in the Atlantic Ocean. We can't possibly be near enough to Egypt to see the Sphinx and Pyramids—"

His voice trailed off at the end of his sentence and became silent, chiefly because there was no use him denying the evidence before his eyes—for with every second the Sphinx and Pyramids were becoming more distinct through the mist. The effect was rendered all the more peculiar by the fact that the glassy ocean seemed to dissolve mysteriously into sand—and within a matter of twenty minutes at the most the *Queen Enid* would definitely drift into that region.

"It's unbelievable!" Commander Rilson declared; and it was just as he had said this that something else happened. The Sphinx and Pyramids disappeared and instead there appeared the unmistakable outlines of New York City.

"Light waves!" Rilson exclaimed, suddenly realising the truth. "Nothing there at all really—just exceptionally vivid mirages. I never saw anything to equal it—"

Neither had lots of other people. At this moment the phenomenon besetting the *Queen Enid* was apparent all over the world. The apparently immutable law that an object must be in a certain place because the light-waves radiating from it say it is so had ceased, like radio waves, to operate. Or if it operated at all it was in a completely disorganised form, just as an image is disturbed in a clear sheet of water when waves cross the pool.

In all parts of the world the law that a thing is so because it can be seen was suddenly at variance. True, the solid believable "get-hold-of" facts remained. One could hold a brick and be sure it was there, whilst the aberrant light-waves said you were holding something else—or even that you were holding nothing at all.

In Australia, where it was still night, the sky was ridden with incredible visions of liners floating upside down in the serene heavens—deflected light-waves from the oceans on the other side of the world. In the daylit hemisphere famous landmarks, which automatically emanated more light-photons than a smaller object, changed position bewilderingly. The Empire State Building, for instance, was declared to be standing in the middle of Clapham Common! On the other hand, Tower Bridge was seen by many Americans to be spanning Broadway.

People, mountains, mice and molehills switched about with bewildering speed, utterly disproving all normal laws. In every case they were found to be but wraiths with no more solidity than a rainbow. Light no longer came direct: it was bent, warped, and refracted as Earth sped further and further into the giant fault in space.. The Earth, as light-waves went even more crazy, was seething with unbearable heat.

From the Tropics tens of thousands of people were streaming, chartering every known means of transport to snatch them away from the roasting griddle that had become the Equator. Here, too, the sun's other radiations were at work—radiations only guessed at in the normal way or detected by instruments. Radiations unseen which blinded hundreds of thousands of men, women and children in the equatorial regions, whilst others were blasted down with a devilish and fatal skin disease which had all the appearance of radiation-burns. The real tragedy of warped space was now commencing really to make itself felt— and none knew how long the horror would continue, for not even science could measure the extent of the warp in space.

CHAPTER FOUR

DEVOLUTION

Whilst the peoples of the world struggled like ants to escape from a bush-fire, Evelyn Woodcroft and Janet Meigan each lay slumped in wicker chairs, legs out-thrust in a most unladylike fashion, arms dangling helplessly over the chairs' sides.

Prayerbook Meigan sat in shirt and trousers beside the table, smoking a cigarette and scowling at the open doorway through which the appalling sunshine blazed. Rivulets of perspiration were coursing down his smooth face.

"God Almighty, I never knew a heat-wave like this!" Mike Woodcroft declared at last, tearing off his sweat-sodden shirt and flinging it to one side. "Or anyway I never knew one to come on so suddenly!"

"'He opened His mouth, and the Earth melted'," Prayerbook observed absently.

Mike swung on him, his eyes hard. "Don't you start spouting Biblical stuff now, Prayerbook, or I'll break your neck! So help me, I'm in no mood to stand for it!"

"Sooner it comes night the better I'll like it," Evelyn remarked lazily, picking up a newspaper and using it as a fan. "This is worse than being on the hot seat: at least you get that over quick."

"It's all so—so unnatural," Janet said, sitting up. "As if everything is burning up. In fact I—"

She frowned as she gazed through the open window, then she got to her feet and went across the bungalow's narrow main room. She withdrew her hand sharply from the sunlit door as it scorched her palm.

"Look over there!" she exclaimed, and pointed to a spot in the hazy distance. Smoke was pluming blackly into the shimmering air.

"Grass fire," Mike growled, coming to her side, his big chest gleaming with sweat. "Can't expect much else in this. We must be hitting the highest temperature ever. Which reminds me—"

He turned to squint at the thermometer and he too sensed the same uneasiness as Janet. The mercury had climbed to 130 degrees Fahrenheit, and even as Mike watched it climbed a little more, edging upwards remorselessly.

"Better keep out of the sunshine, Jan," Evelyn advised. "It might do things to you. We've enough on our hands for later on without a sunstroke case added, to it."

With a nod Janet turned back into the room. Mike mooched after her, playing in his memory with the newspaper facts Prayerbook had read out on the journey from town. Something about a fault in space—which didn't mean a thing to a killer with the brutish instincts of Mike Woodcroft. All he knew was that he felt as if he were being fried.

"For the love of Pete—"

Prayerbook uttered the words in a sudden yell and jumped to his feet so violently that his chair went spinning backwards. The two girls and Mike swung to question him, then they stopped in awe as they realised what had smitten him. The sunlight was commencing to shine through the roof!

It was not burning through it: it was simply that light waves normally blocked by the thinnest of solids were now going through them instead! By slow degrees, like cloud vapourising from before a bright globe, the sun merged through the wooden roof, first in the outline of a misted blur—then it became round, and finally its rays blasted clean through with a brilliance which was bewildering.

At the same moment there was a gigantic shifting and changing of ordinary values. Shadows melted, solids became quite transparent. Light was everywhere—blinding, inexorable.

It affected everything and everybody on Earth and in the Solar System at the same moment. Solids were no longer blocking light as Earth hurtled onwards through the Warp.

Mike Woodcraft flung his arm up over his face and then dropped it again in stunned amazement. His arm did not shut out the glare! He could still see the sun. So could Prayerbook and so could the two girls. If they covered their faces, if they shut their eyes, the sun remained, pouring an intolerable effulgence upon them.

"What's gone wrong?" Evelyn demanded in a shriek, springing up. "Why does the sun shine through us instead of on us? What in hell's happened?"

"How should I know?" Mike snarled at her.

"'And the Moon shall be as the Sun, and the Sun shall increase sevenfold'," Prayerbook whispered.

"Oh, shut up!" Evelyn spat at him. "This is a fine time to come out with that stuff! Things have gone that cockeyed I think we should get out—"

"Why?" Janet asked quietly. "What good would it do us?"

"Because in case you've forgotten it there's a grass fire over there—you pointed it out yourself—and I can't see any earthly reason why everything around us shouldn't go up in flames at any moment! Look at that thermometer!"

It registered 133 degrees Fahrenheit..

"We're staying!" Mike decided roughly, and catching Evelyn by the arm he whirled her back into her chair. As she sat blinking at his massive body she was conscious of an amazing fact: she could see through him! His spinal column, his ribs, and his legs were etched out against the glare of the sun as though on an X-ray plate.

"We're staying until tonight because we've got to," Mike added. "Because you've gone jittery over some hocus-pocus with the sun there's no reason why we should start running and sticking our necks in a noose. I don't have to remind you that we did a job in town, do I, and that the police are not exactly a bunch of idiots?"

"Night—" Janet repeated, wincing and turning her face from the light—only to look into more blazing glare saturating and piercing every molecule in the room. "Night! What a relief that will be when it comes."

"Since it's six hours away yet we can get used to this," Mike said, looking at his wristwatch. "If you two girls want to go in the bedroom and lie down I'm not stopping you."

"Who wants to lie down?" Evelyn demanded, wiping her face with a sodden handkerchief. "Do you think we can't stick it?"

"I just wonder," Prayerbook said, slowly, narrowing his eyes in the glare, "where this is going to finish? You two girls and Mike here haven't got my education. You don't know much about science."

"Neither do you," Mike sneered, going across to the bar.

"Not in a big way, true," Prayerbook agreed, sitting back in his chair, "but I'm not so dumb that I can't see that this is a disaster of the first magnitude. Heat beyond endurance, light going through solids as though they're glass! It never happened before—not that we know of. It might even be the end of the world. It says somewhere—'And the very stones shall be consumed—'"

"Aren't things bad enough?" Janet cried tearfully. "Be quiet, or else talk sense!"

"All right, kid, all right—you've got nerves," Prayerbook sympathised. "Not that I blame you—but nerves aren't going to get us out of this mess."

There was silence for a moment. Though there were only four of them, though they had arrived at this bungalow quite calmly with their plans well laid; they were commencing to suffer from the abnormal and prolonged strain. They did not know it, but it was quite the logical outcome of the weird change in basic laws and the consequent wrench on the nervous system.

In city and hamlet, in the air and on the sea, amongst every type of man, woman and child, it was the same. Now Earth was near the centre of the space-warp every known law of physics was in the discard. Radio waves were unintelligible—a scrambled mass of static; X-rays refused to function properly; light went through solids; the sun's radiations themselves had taken on a new rate of vibration which made the visible spectrum alter its frequency. Because of this, light in particular had taken on the penetrative power of X-rays, which in most cases was responsible for the plague of blindness and skin disease already striding across the Earth.

The heat too was an added menace, and was not confined to any one part of the world. It soaked in everywhere from Pole to Pole, thawing Arctic and Antarctic and turning the equatorial regions to unendurable hell!

* * * * * * *

In Annex 10 in the Adirondack Mountains the temperature registered 134 degrees Fahrenheit, and was still rising. Dr. Gray and his fellow scientists were all stripped to the waist, towels round their necks with which they constantly mopped their streaming faces. They had already discovered that the sun was shining directly at them even through the rock ledge that protected the roof, and the instruments they handled registered a grim story. Cosmic rays, X-rays, and a while host of ultra-short-waved radiations were pouring in from the unmasked solar photosphere.

"Where this is going to finish I don't dare to think," Dr. Gray whispered at last, staggering up from his chair. "There must be tens of thousands of people being affected by these radiations— to what extent depends upon their constitution. The cosmic rays must also be affecting all the protoplasmic forms of life and stimulating them as never before. The heat added to the stimulation will enable them to grow. In all parts of the world tremendous mutations must be occurring—and we can't get a single word about it with the damned radio out of action."

"There are carrier pigeons in the basement," Sheldon remarked. "Any use sending one of those and see if we can get in touch with somebody?"

Dr. Gray debated for a moment or two and then shook his head. "Be a waste of time, I'm afraid. I doubt if any bird could survive more than a few minutes outside. Though radiations are driving straight through matter the matter does make a slight protection. Outside there will be none at all—"

He broke off sharply as one of the scientists who had been busily making calculations suddenly slumped out of his chair and crashed heavily to the floor. He did not remain inert, however: instead he held his head desperately and shouted in sudden anguish.

Immediately the other scientists rushed to his assistance, lifting his writhing body preparatory to carrying it to the adjoining bedrooms section. But they were not quick enough. By the time they had raised him his convulsive movements ceased and it was quite obvious that he was dead.

"Put him on the floor," Dr. Gray instructed, set-faced. "If we can find out what happened to him maybe we can save ourselves from a similar fate: Obviously radiation got him, but we'll try and find out where. Sheldon, bring in the surgical readers."

Sheldon nodded and hurried away. In a moment or two he returned from an adjoining compartment, pushing before him a rubber-tyred trolley upon which stood all manner of technical instruments, specially designed for reading any portion of the human body.

Gray switched on the self-contained batteries and held the "pick-up" over the dead scientist's body. The images it picked up were transmitted to the scanning screen in a semi X-ray fashion, but the fault in the ether made the image hazy and indistinct.

"It would be!" Gray muttered in subdued fury. "If we can only determine what part of the body the radiations affect—whether it be the brain or the heart—we might even be able to devise something to offset them."

With the rest of the scientists he stared intently at the screen, meanwhile adjusting the focusing screws, but no matter how hard he strove the light-photons would not behave. The image danced, wavered, covered itself in weird snaky traceries, and at length was lost in a common haze.

"No use, sir," Sheldon said finally. "This instrument is as crazy as everything else. I'm afraid we'll never know what hit Meadows—or at any rate we won't know exactly where. I imagine it must have been his brain which was attacked."

Gray nodded absently and Sheldon pushed away the trolley. Mopping themselves freely the scientists looked down at their dead comrade, then at Dr. Gray.

"If we had lead helmets we might save ourselves," one the men suggested. "Cosmic rays are blocked by lead."

"If we were only dealing in cosmic rays I'd agree," Gray answered, "but the instruments, those of them which still work reasonably, show that we are dealing with wavelengths even shorter than cosmic, against which there is no known protection. Not even lead. Besides, since this spatial fault makes even light-waves pass through solids I think we can assume that cosmic rays would go through lead at the moment."

"Then we stay here and risk the same thing happening to us as happened to Meadows?" Sheldon asked bitterly.

"We're scientists," Gray reminded him quietly. "It is for us to stick at our jobs until we can do it no longer. Those who survive this catastrophe will need every record they can get concerning it, if only to prepare in case it should ever happen again."

"The radiations up on this mountain height are probably far worse than at the surface," Sheldon pointed out. "In our effort to isolate ourselves maybe we cut our own throats. It's an obvious fact that with every foot we go up from the ground the percentage of radiation from outer space increases. Possibly that is why we're in such danger."

"Yes—possibly." Gray made the admission as though it had only just occurred to him—which in truth it had. "And if that be so, what is the answer? We cannot leave here."

"I think you should speak for yourself there, Dr. Gray," Sheldon snapped. "We may be scientists and we may have a duty to perform, but life comes before everything. I, for one, am not prepared to sacrifice my life for science or anything else. Things have got to the pitch where the only law is that of self-preservation."

The scientists looked at one another uncomfortably, then two of them crossed to Sheldon's side. The others, older men most of them, remained with Dr. Gray.

"You two gentlemen feel the same way?" Gray asked quietly, studying the two men ranged beside Sheldon.

"Afraid we do, sir," one of them answered. "Meaning no disrespect to you."

Gray smiled wryly. "And now you have come to this decision what do you propose doing? You are scientists: you must realise that in attempting to leave this Annex you will expose your-selves to worse danger than that which exists inside it."

"We'll take that chance," Sheldon said stubbornly. "I am convinced it is only our altitude here which is causing us to get the radiations so severely. I'm all for using our single plane to make an attempt to reach ground level—"

"About time you star-gazers got some sense!"

The scientists turned as the pain-congested voice reached them. Absorbed in their own dilemma they had forgotten .all about Woodstock J. Holmes who had gone off to the sleeping quarters. He stood now in the doorway that led to them, .his eyes bloodshot, sweat gleaming on his fleshy, naked chest.

"We should have got out of here long ago," he added, looking towards the dead man on the floor. "Or was it him who suddenly made you see reason—? God, my head's killing me! And the heat!"

The financier staggered a little then got control over himself again. Strong as a bull he was, and it was amazing how much he could endure without going under.

"Well, what sort of a decision have you arrived at?" he demanded, moving unsteadily forward. "Or have you arrived at one at all?"

"We're leaving," Sheldon answered. "We three here. We might stand a chance at ground level. Dr. Gray has elected to stay on."

"Because of the two dangers it is the lesser," Gray said quietly.

"That's a matter of opinion!" Holmes snapped. "I'd have gone long ago. In fact we all would if you'd had the blasted sense to listen to me! All right, come on. Sooner the better!"

He swung to the door, but before he reached it he detoured abruptly and from the wall-rack snatched down a loaded revolver, kept there in case of any possible emergency. The scientists stared at him in surprise, particularly the three who had been about to follow him.

"What's the idea, Mr. Holmes?" Sheldon demanded, his eyes narrowed. "You don't need that."

"Maybe I think differently!" the financier retorted. "It just occurs to me that there's only one plane here and it won't carry more than two people. If we risk four we're liable to crash."

"We'll make it—somehow," Sheldon insisted.

"I don't intend to take the risk. I must get away from here, if only to see how my various interests are faring. With you men it's your job to be here. And don't any of you try and stop me!"

Nobody did try because a loaded revolver was too dangerous a weapon with which to argue. The financier backed out of the doorway and so into the shimmering blaze outside. He stood for a moment revealed in X-ray fashion, then he slammed the door and darted across to where the plane stood on the specially prepared runway flattened into the rockery. Back in the Annex, Sheldon and his two colleagues made a dive to follow, then they paused at Dr. Gray's sharp voice.

"Before you got out there, my friends, take a look through this window! What can happen to Holmes can happen also to you. Make your choice—"

Puzzled, Sheldon slowed his pace and gave a glance at his comrades—then he moved to the window and peered outside. His breath caught sharply in horrified astonishment. In grim silence he and the other scientists watched the fate overtaking the financier in his desperate bid for "freedom."

He staggered as he walked across the sizzling stretch of bare rock between the Annex and the plane. Though the sunlight was shining through the Annex roof there was, nonetheless, a misty protection that was entirely absent outside. So Woodstock J. Holmes received the full blast of radiations at this high altitude in the Adirondacks, and things happened to him even as he moved. His staggering became a pronounced stoop and his running changed to a waddle. As he moved, his knuckles occasionally touched the ground. It seemed incredible, but by the time he had reached the plane—only to recoil from it as he touched its blistering surface—his chest and back had become covered in fine hair.

"What the devil's happening to him?" Sheldon demanded, his voice strained.

"Devolution," Gray answered curtly. "The one result I expected from the sun. He's going back down the evolutive scale—"

He did not need to add any further explanation for the situation outside explained itself with every ghastly second. Holmes was clawing helplessly at the burning-hot door of the, plane's cabin, and failing to open it, probably because his :brain had already retrograded so far that he could not understand the lock.

He sank to his knees, a hairy, crouching figure, his "paws" clawing at the searing rocks. For an instant there was a vision of his face, hair grown low down on his forehead, the nose curiously flattened and the mouth jutting. In less than five minutes Woodstock J. Holmes, mastermind of Wall Street, had become something allied to a Cro-Magnon man.

"What—what do we do to help him?" Sheldon asked uncertainly.

"Nothing!" Gray's voice was curt. "Even if we risked our lives by going outside it wouldn't do any good. In this short time a blast of radiations, cosmic and other ultra-short lengths, has undone the evolutionary work of countless centuries. We just have to leave him."

It was not callousness on Dr. Gray's part: just plain commonsense. And in any case it was apparent by now from his motionless attitude that Holmes was dead—or very soon would be from lying in that ghastly heat unprotected from the flood of radiations.

"Well, gentlemen?" Gray asked dryly. "Do you still wish to depart?"

Sheldon looked uncomfortable. "I'm sorry, Dr. Gray," he apologised. "I'm afraid I lost my head for the time being. In my own defence I can only say that I can hardly be blamed."

"We still have our work to do," Gray said, turning back to the instruments. "We must, if we possibly can, chart how long this is going to last, or devise some method of overcoming the danger of radiation."

"Temperature's gone up two more degrees," Sheldon announced, studying the thermometer. "One hundred and thirty-six and still rising. Honestly, Doctor, we can't stand much more."

"Until that point has been reached we must do all we can," Gray replied, as immovably the leader as ever. "Now our little disagreement is at an end, gentlemen, please return to your posts. We'll have to work things out so that we can operate in shifts— though rest is next to impossible in this blazing sunlight."

Sheldon sat down slowly and wiped his streaming face and chest, then he looked puzzled. "There's one thing I don't under-stand, Dr. Gray. How is it that Holmes should be attacked like that outside, and yet we in here are not? Even poor Meadows, back on the floor there, didn't devolve even though he died."

Gray glanced towards the corpse that had now been drawn up close by the wall and covered with a tarpaulin sheeting. "I have only one explanation to offer," he said at length. "This Annex is, of course, directly under an overhanging ledge of rock. It is possible that, though light waves are able to penetrate it at the moment, the very short ones responsible for devolu-tion are not—not in any great quantity anyway. The rock also contains lead, which must act as a natural deflector. Out there, where the unfortunate Holmes is lying, there is no protection whatever—and we see the result."

"Then what killed Meadows?" another of the men asked.

"Possibly radiations; possibly heat-stroke. We were not able to discover—" Gray turned back impatiently to the instruments. "Gentlemen, we are wasting our time on idle conjectures and we have other things to do. How are your instruments behaving, Mr. Sheldon?"

"Fairly well, sir. The light photometer shows a deflection of half a circumference. That, translated into ordinary terms, means an apparent shift of image over dozens of miles in some cases."

"Which will mean mirages wherever the deflection occurs," Gray said. "Possibly it will be most noticeable over the open sea and large tracts of desert areas. As for the rest of these instruments, recording ultraviolet, infrared, and so forth, they seem to be utterly out of action. They just don't make sense." Gray clenched his fist. "If only radio were operating and we could get some information from other parts of the world. As it is we can only record what we observe and pool our results afterwards with the other experts."

"Granting there is ever an end to this hideousness," Sheldon commented gloomily.

"I remain convinced that there must be," Gray insisted: "A flaw in the ether surely can't be infinite in extent, any more than a rainstorm can last forever? It is only a phase, and an extremely dangerous and uncomfortable one, but it must end somewhere."

"If it doesn't kill us in the process," Sheldon sighed. "Maybe we'll get some better idea when night comes and we can take a look at the heavens—providing the light-waves are straight enough to make observation possible."

"Unless we're out of the flaw by night it just won't help us," Gray said quietly. "We're doomed, I'm afraid, to an eternal day! Don't you realise that, since the sun is shining through solids, there is no reason why it shouldn't shine clean through Earth itself? That's why I wish we could get in touch with Australia, so that we can discover how they are faring. The old saying may be true—the sun never sets!"

* * * * * * *

Even if the sun was not actually setting it was certainly lower in the sky, particularly in Sussex where Martin Horsley was at the close of the largest meal he had eaten in years. Here it was towards nine o'clock in the evening, Sussex being some five hours ahead of New York time. Since four o'clock the heat had been climbing degree by degree, which in itself was fantastic as, normally, the heat abates as the evening advances. This time no such thing had happened and the diagonal rays of the late June sun were blasting through the trees around the hotel, and straight through the walls and roof.

Not that Martin Horsley seemed worried. He was in an exceptionally genial mood, smiling to himself over the empty plates in the private dining room, regardless of the shafts of light blinding and stabbing at him from every side. He was possibly the only man in the hotel who was fully dressed. In other directions the management and staff were prostrate, striving in vain to shield themselves from the glare, swilling down drinks so constantly that they thought they would float away.

The only other person in the room with Horsley was the faithful Dawson, still in shirtsleeves, and Horsley was in far too pleasant a temper to demand that his factotum should wear a full uniform.

"This, Dawson, is the most wonderful day in the history of the world!" Horsley declared presently, pushing back his chair and rising to his feet. "If it has done for other unfortunate souls what it has done for me then the day will be remembered as one of blessing."

"I rather think, sir, that your reaction is exceptional," Dawson remarked weakly. "The rest of the people in this hotel are completely laid out with the heat. Some of them are complaining of violent headaches, too."

"Headaches? Bah!" Horsley spread his arms and then thudded his clenched fists against his chest. "They should do as I have done—eat a thundering good meal and enjoy the warmth. Never in my life have I been so comfortable. We've been to many places, you and I, Dawson, looking for warmth. Persian Gulf, the Sudan, Morocco, California—but we never found it until today."

"Yes, sir, I quite agree," Dawson muttered, dabbing his face. "And the temperature's still rising. Last time I looked at it in the hall it was a hundred and thirty. I can't understand how you thrive on it, sir!"

"You would if you'd always been as cold as me! But it isn't just that, Dawson," Horsley continued, musing. "It's a complete change in the mental outlook. I don't feel at all like the same ailing man who came into this hotel earlier today. I felt then as I have always felt—that I might die any minute and be glad to go. But now! Why, the very zest of life is upon me. I want to work, and walk, and leap, and struggle! Bounding energy, Dawson! Bounding energy!"

This time Dawson did not say anything: he was beyond it. The metamorphosis of Martin Horsley was quite beyond him—as much as it was beyond Horsley himself. Since Horsley was not a scientist—nor was his factotum—he was not capable of under-standing that the ultra-short waves penetrating to Earth were having a remarkable effect upon his nervous system. Whereas they over-stimulated and killed human beings in perfect health—or else devolved them, as in the case of Woodstock J. Holmes—there were many instances similar to Horsley's where invalids had responded to the stimulus in a different fashion and suddenly found glowing health and vigour. Horsley and Holmes were but two examples of one particular wavelength killing in one instance and restoring in another, so haphazard is Nature in the bestowal of her curses and blessings.

"Soon be sunset," Horsley commented, crossing to the window and looking out quite unconcerned into the blazing diagonal glare. "Take a look at that scene, Dawson! Did you ever see anything so magnificent? Like a flood of gold! I could laugh when I recall how we were warned of all sorts of horrors to come and instead we get only beauty. Even the trees are swallowed up in the radiance."

"I shouldn't stand in the direct eye of that sunlight, sir," Dawson warned. "It might do things to you."

"Only good things, Dawson, believe me," Martin Horsley smiled. "There is beneficence, health, and power in that light outside. I even feel minded to go for a walk to the village and back."

"It's a risk, sir," Dawson insisted.

"Nonsense, man! You don't have to come with me if you feel afraid. I'll be all right."

Dawson, who always felt it his responsibility to look after Horsley's well being, made another vague protest but Horsley would not listen. Singing cheerfully to himself he strode from the dining room and went upstairs for his hat.

Five minutes later he came downstairs again, stick in his hand and hat on his head. In some surprise he looked at the proprietor, drenched in perspiration, lolling on his reception desk.

"What's the matter, my friend?" Horsley chuckled. "Feeling warm?"

"I'm—I'm dying, Mr. Horsley. Honest I am." The proprietor breathed hard and pointed a shaky finger towards the thermometer. "Look at that mercury! One hundred and thirty-two! It's more than flesh and blood can stand!"

"Nonsense, man. You're just out of condition, that's all. Look at me! Never fitter. Anyway, I'll be back for supper."

"Supper?" the proprietor repeated blankly. "You actually mean you are going to eat a supper after that huge meal?"

Horsley nodded calmly. "Certainly! Think of the years I've lived on peptonised rubbish! Time I made up for it, isn't it?"

The proprietor was too dumbfounded to make any further comment, so Horsley went cheerfully on his way, striding out into the low rays of the intolerable sun as it hung just clear of the horizon.

Horsley, despite the tremendous emotional and physical stimulation he had received, was nonetheless conscious of the vast, impalpable difference in everything. Normally at this hour the birds should have been singing their last song before nesting; there should have been purple mists couched to catch the sun for the night; the sky should have been mistily blue with here and there a star peeping out of advancing twilight.

Not one of these aspects of a summer evening in England was evident. Instead, once he got beyond the shimmering blaze of sunlight and trees around the hotel, Horsley found himself alone in the lane. Here the sun was shining straight at him, a titanic flooding golden ball ahead, and though a quarter of it was below the horizon it didn't somehow seem to make any difference. The horizon might have been. composed of water for all the solidity it presented.

To a man in a less incredibly exalted state than Horsley the evening would have struck terror. Not a soul in sight; the empty lane leading straight down to a village which looked mysteriously lit from behind, with no shadows anywhere. It seemed to Horsley as he progressed that he was in a world suddenly made of glass where everything was transparent. Once he looked straight into the eye of the bewildering sun and then wished he hadn't. He felt something stir painfully at the back of his brain and for a second or two his sense of fantastic well being wavered—then as quickly returned. Stimulation! Stimulation! With every moment that the sun soaked its fifth-octave radiations into him he was being transformed—but a human body can only absorb so much stimulus, and then....

Ten minutes of brisk walking brought Horsley to the village and by this time the sun should have been below the horizon. Perhaps it was. Horsley could not exactly tell. He stood alone in the centre of the village street, trying to picture the people within the semi-transparent houses. He stood alone, a wondering man, impressed by the fantastic power of Nature when she behaves contrary to rule.

The sun had set, yes: there was no doubt of that—if by setting is meant that the sun is below the horizon. But to Horsley it appeared that the sun was still shining at him obliquely from somewhere below with those searing, blinding rays. He held up his free left hand for a moment to cover his eyes and saw the bones of his fingers lined starkly against his flesh.

This was enough for Horsley. He turned his back abruptly on the blinding orb and began to trace his way down the lane towards the hotel. It occurred to him as he went that untended cattle were still in the fields, cows chiefly, most of them moaning pitifully and all of them with their backs to the glare. No birds sang and the leafy trees were deathly still, touched by the satanic golden flood that should long since have subsided into night.

"There is no night," Horsley whispered to himself. "No night any more. Just day—and light—and strength!"

But *was* there strength? He was not quite so convinced of it now as he had been. That stupendous energy and exaltation which had propelled him out of the hotel to indulge in this amazing walk was not quite so obvious now. In fact the great barrier of Earth, masking many of the sun's radiations even though his light was practically unshielded, was automatically cutting off the rejuvenating wavelengths that had raised Horsley from the depths of invalidism to the heights of well being. He was still vigorous—even hungry—but the zenith had been reached, and passed. And as it was for him, so it was for the tens of thousands who had likewise been affected.

He returned to the hotel in a far less exuberant mood, and the moment he entered the main hallway he stopped in astonishment, faced with a scene almost as fantastic as that which existed outside.

The proprietor and one or two members of his family were slumped helplessly on tables and chairs, overcome by the raging heat. Behind them, seeming as though it were centred just below the base of the main wall, loomed the overpowering circle of the sun. Against this, swirling about the hall and up and down the stairway in clouds, were bats. Hundreds of them, and their numbers rapidly increasing, the air thick with the leathery rustle of their wings.

"What the devil!" Horsley exploded, and his exclamation brought the tottering, sweat-drenched figure of Dawson from the lounge. He was dripping wet, wearing only shorts, and clutched .a massive poker in his hand.

"I've been trying to get rid of these beastly things, sir!" he panted. "They seem to have come from the old belfry at the top of the building—probably driven out by the fact that night hasn't come as it should. It's ten o'clock and the sun's still shining."

"I can see that," Horsley snorted. "Bats! Filthy things! Here—I'll help you."

"Mind how you do it, sir. They bite. Look at me—"

Dawson put forth his arms and there were distinct blood specks upon them where he had been nipped.

"I think they're crazy, frantic," he said. "They can't make head or tail of what's happened to everything—not that I can myself."

"We need help," Horsley gasped, as three of the hats flew dangerously near his face. "Why the hell isn't the proprietor doing something? Wake him up!"

"No use, sir," Dawson muttered. "He's dead. So are these two servants—and in the upper rooms his wife and daughter are also dead."

Horsley said nothing for the moment. This sudden wholesale wiping out of everybody living was sobering in the extreme. "Why?" he asked abruptly. "What killed them? You're all right, and I know I am."

"I feel about all in, sir," Dawson muttered, swaying as he spoke. "The temperature is a hundred and thirty-six and I'm pretty nearly at the end of my rope. That battle I had with the bats nearly finished me."

Horsley looked at them swirling around in the maddening golden light. "Bit you?" he repeated. "Why should they? These aren't the South American vampires: just long-eared English bats. Harmless."

"Harmless normally, yes—but at present they're as crazy as anything else. If we're going to stay here—and I suppose we are if only for protection—we've got to be rid of them. Look out!" Dawson finished hoarsely, and made a terrific swipe with the poker as a bat flew straight for Horsley's face.

He jerked on one side, lashing out with his walking stick at the same time. The bat collapsed under the blow it received and this seemed to stir some kind of vindictive kinship amongst its fellows.

The hordes descended, black as autumn leaves against the diagonal sunshine and within seconds Horsley and Dawson found themselves engaged in the most incredible battle ever. They could not know it, but the curious sixth sense of a bat had been disturbed the world over, and the chaos of Nature had turned their natures completely round. They were savagely dangerous and were anything but confined to this lonely hotel. The sweltering countryside was thick with them, and everywhere they went they attacked, whether their prey were bird, animal, or human.

They came from the belfry above the hotel; they came from the open back and front doors; they came in their hundreds and then in their thousands—and with them there also arrived myriads of curious stinging gnats, mysteriously evolved "midges" armed now with venomous stings. Horsley and Dawson hardly had the chance to realize what had hit them so thick did the choking air become with the hurtling pests. They were everywhere, festooning the walls, pecking at the dead bodies lying in various parts of the hallway, blacking out the glare of the sun at intervals, or else hanging in front of it in X-ray formation.

In seven minutes of bitter fighting with the poker Dawson was spent. He could struggle no more. With a hopeless, dazed look on his face he dropped his weapon, staggered and winced under the myriad cuts and stabs he received, and at last he crashed over on his face.

"Dawson, you fool!" Horsley yelled, lashing around him. "Don't die on me now, man! Get up!"

Dawson did not get up. He was definitely finished, his body already disappearing under the dark clouds of bats and insects. Horsley gave one glance at him then his own stupendous energy rose to a final surge. He had to get out of this hotel: that seemed the only way. Better to be outside in the unnatural day-night than penned in here with these! So, he started fighting for the front doorway, battering and slashing defiantly as he went—but the more he fought the thicker the hordes descended upon him and the more he felt his strength failing.

It couldn't fail! It mustn't! He had risen to such heights of health and vigour it couldn't let him down now—but it did, completely. With the vital radiations no longer reaching him from the sun, blocked by the various metals and veins of which Earth herself is composed, Horsley was running down like a clock with a failing mainspring.

His efforts became weaker. He stumbled and fell flat on his face. His life went out under the thickening cloud of bats and insects that surged relentlessly about him.

CHAPTER FIVE
FIRST CONTACT

But surely it was in the equatorial regions where the full fantastic effect of the flaw in the fabric of space was most noticeable, those regions directly in line with the sun and in the thick of his mysteriously changed wavelengths.

In his African bungalow Henry Brand, the crooked trader, drank all the whiskey he could consume following his wild dash out of the jungle after upbraiding M'Bonga and his tribesmen. He was quivering, half drunk, staring with smarting eyes into a sunlight which was now blasting down through the trees and the vegetational roof of his 'home'. It did not make sense to him that plants and lichens should be growing whilst he watched them: it made even less sense for the sun to be shining through solid branches and leaves. Everything was crazy—everything.

As for M'Bonga and his tribesmen, they were quite convinced by now that the white man had overdone his magic. The heat was beyond anything even an African could stand, climbing up to the 180 degrees mark, sapping life out of the natives as they stared in paralysed wonder at a glare which seared into their very brains. For some reason they did not look in the opposite direction: sheer fascination compelled them to stare into that golden glory, with the inevitable result that presently things grew dim around them and the silently swaying and growing vegetation was no longer as clearly visible as it had been.

"Bwana, he did this!" M'Bonga cried presently, dragging his gaze away from the glare. "He make lord of day hot—to fry us, he said. We kill! Bwana try to kill us! We kill him instead."

His fellow tribesmen growled assent and rose to their feet. Each one had been kneeling, staring into the blaze. Now they came to look at the bungalow it appeared darkly shadowed and already disappearing under a riot of fast-growing vegetation. For the jungle men to understand what scientific twist had caused the sudden tremendous surge in vegetational life was impossible: they could not know—and neither could the whiskey-sodden, brutish Henry Brand—that the wavelengths responsible for mutation were at their maximum on the equator, hence vegetation was speeding ahead at nearly ten times the normal rate—growing, flowering, dying, and re-growing all in the space of minutes. That the radiations had not acted on the human being was surprising—but it had a scientific explanation. Devolution was possible, as it had happened in the case of Woodstock J. Holmes, but its delay was caused by the density of the atmosphere at the equator. High in the Adirondack Mountains the rarification had been the main cause of devolution: here it was less apparent, but it was there insofar as all normal instincts had by now deserted the natives and Henry Brand. Their natures had already sunk to the level of the beast.

That M'Bonga and his tribesmen were bent on the murder of Brand was obvious, but before they could even reach the bungalow the after-effects of their prolonged staring into the blinding sunlight began to have its effect.

The shadows appeared to them to deepen—but in truth there were no shadows, not anywhere on Earth at that moment. The shadows were the first streaks of blindness creeping upon the eyes of the tribesmen, and within a few minutes the process was complete. The deadly radiations had seared all trace of sight from their eyes and they found themselves blundering into chaotic darkness and furious heat.

By all the pagan gods he knew M'Bonga cursed Henry Brand, his vilifying voice reaching the trader as he half lay on the table with an empty whiskey glass in his hand.

He looked up and frowned, a half snarl on his thick lips.

Then, drunk though he was, he reeled to his feet and grabbed at his stock whip, determined to teach the natives the lesson of their lives. He strode to the doorway and then reeled back dumbfounded, his view completely blocked by an incredible profusion of vegetation.

"M'Bonga, where are you?" he demanded thickly. "When I get this whip across your hide, you scum, I'll—"

He stopped, his eyes narrowed as he caught sight of the head boy for a moment in the saturating glare. He was blundering around helplessly, feeling his way amongst the expanding bushes whilst behind him the rest of the natives were crouched, cursing the dark fluently in their native tongue.

"Dark?" Brand repeated to himself, puzzled. "What the hell are they talking about? Couldn't be brighter!"

Then as the truth dawned upon him his eyes glinted with sadistic satisfaction. So the lazy devils couldn't see, eh? Well, that made his task all the easier. They had dared to curse him in every way they knew and for that there had to be an answer—and a ruthless one. He gripped his whip more tightly and made his uncertain way down the steps.

But before he could reach M'Bonga things happened, so swiftly he had no time to measure them. In his intoxicated state he did not see the javelin-barb which was developing straight ahead of him, swelling and expanding with every second—a monstrous, hypertrophied thorn of nearly two feet in length.

Brand saw it when it was too late. He charged towards M'Bonga, his whip upraised—and at the same instant he saw the thorn. Frantically though he tried to check his onrush he was not quick enough. The point went clean into his heart, impaling him as though with a spear. A gurgle escaped him and the whip dropped from his hand.

M'Bonga, feeling his way around helplessly in the darkness, heard the thud of a body—and then silence. He stood wondering and listening—then again he screamed against the pagan gods that had deprived him of the power of sight.

* * * * * *

Samuel Baines stirred weakly and rubbed the back of his head. It ached abominably, and his fingers encountered a fair-sized lump, which, however, was apparently not bleeding.

"Dad—you all right?" He recognised the voice as Bertie's, sharp with anxiety.

"Yes, I'm all right." Samuel Baines staggered to his feet in the darkness. "What about you? And Gwen?"

"Gwen's sprained her ankle," Bertie said.

"But I can hop, if that's any good," Gwen herself added.

"Well, anyway, we're in one piece—which is about the only thing to be thankful for at the moment. What on earth possessed the pair of you to come down here?"

"We didn't come down, Dad—we fell down." Bertie was doing his best to sound contrite. "We wanted to explore and—well, it was Gwen's silly fault. She slipped over the edge of the pathway above and dropped down here. I scrambled down to help her with no idea of how I'd get back—so we just stuck. We had Gwen's torch, until the battery gave out. Then just as we were getting scared we heard you and Mum calling, thank heaven."

"I'll tan the pair of you when we get out of this," Samuel Baines muttered. "When we get out! Your mother's gone for help and that may take some time."

He had hardly made the statement when there came a cry from far above, as though Claire, for it was her voice, was trying to get her bearings.

"Sam! Sam, where are you?"

"Right here!" he yelled back. "You're too far to the right from the sound of things. What's the matter?"

There was the sound of hurrying feet in the stones above, then Claire's voice sounded from a position directly overhead. "It's no use my trying to get a search-party, Sam. There's something wrong outside."

"Wrong? Wrong? What on earth do you mean?"

"It's so appallingly hot! I couldn't possibly survive above a few minutes. The thermometer at the cave entrance registers over a hundred and it's three miles to the nearest place to get help. I can't do it, Sam!"

"Well, that's a nice thing to tell me! What are the kids and I supposed to do? Sit here in the dark and wait for pennies from heaven?"

"I don't know what to do." Claire's voice was desperate. "Honest I don't!"

Samuel Baines thought for a moment, then made up his mind. "Can you find your way to the main cavern?" he asked. "The one we were exploring when we found the kids weren't with us?"

"I don't see why not. What then?"

"There must be some people there: we can't be the only ones exploring this confounded place. Ask them for help. What we need most is a rope and some light—'specially light. See what you can do."

"Okay!" agreed Claire, hurrying into the distance.

After a long interval Bertie spoke in a queer voice. "Dad, what's that?"

"Huh? What?" His father started in the darkness and looked around him. "What's what? I don't see anything."

But after a while he did see something—a grotesque, hazy golden circle hanging high in the darkness above the ledge. At the moment it was so dim as to be almost an illusion, but with the seconds it gathered strength until it was tangibly a golden ball.

"What is it?" Gwen gasped, startled. "Looks like an electric globe of some kind."

Samuel Baines had no immediate response to make. He was conscious of the fact that into the abyss in which he and the children stood there was coming a vague suggestion of light. The utter blackness was turning to grey and there were the dimly visible signs of rocks etching themselves out in the advancing murk.

"For the love of Mike, it's the sun!" Samuel Baines gasped at last, and he could hardly believe his own words. "It can't be anything else!"

"That's silly, Dad!" Gwen reproved him. "It can't possibly be the sun. How could it shine through tons of rock?"

"I don't know—but it is doing. And it's infernally hot too! Let's see—what time is it?"

By this time the light had become strong enough for Samuel Baines to distinguish the hands on his wristwatch.

He looked at them, thought for a moment, and then snapped his fingers.

"It's that space business!" he exclaimed. "It's nearly five o'clock, and that space business was supposed to happen around four. It looks as though it has! That must account for the high temperature outside, and for us seeing the sun in here."

"Could space being wrong do that?" Bertie asked, puzzled.

"Course it could," Gwen answered, though she did not sound particularly sure of herself.

"Neither of you kids can be expected to understand this matter," their fadier told them. "I hardly understand it myself, but I suppose that if ether goes funny it might do lots of things to the things that travel through—or on—it, light, for instance. Anyway, that's the sun, and look where we are!"

By this time they might have been outside in the full sunlight for all the difference there was. The roof of the cavern had vanished in a blaze of golden brilliance and the light was beating everywhere. The three appraised their position and discovered they were perched nearly a hundred feet above a sheer drop. Below there loomed ugly spires of rock. Above, a seemingly interminable distance, was the edge of the pathway.

"Thank heaven for this ledge," Samuel Baines muttered, with a little shudder. "If any of us had missed it—"

He left his sentence unfinished, imagination supplying the rest; then at sounds above him he looked up sharply to behold a diagonal view of his wife, remote, hurrying along with a coil of rope in her hand.

"I got one!" she cried, her voice echoing, "but I never would have seen it but for this light being switched on. Wonder who did it? I can't see any people about. The rope was hanging on a hook in a crevice and a notice said 'For Emergency Use'. I suppose I did right taking it?"

"If this isn't an emergency I don't know what is," Samuel Baines retorted. "Throw the rope down quick and make it fast up there."

Claire did as she was bidden and the rope came snaking down into the abyss.

"I'll go first," Samuel Baines said, "then I can haul you two up. You come next, Gwen, and don't try using that ankle of yours. It's as swollen as a pudding."

"Yes, Dad."

Muttering uncomplimentary things about exploring caves, Samuel Baines grabbed the rope and pulled himself up the rocky face like an amateur mountaineer. By the time he had reached the top he was panting hard and perspiring. Claire looked at him in concern, then grabbed him in her arms.

"Thank heaven, Sam—oh, thank heaven! You're sure you're all right?"

"Except for a lump like a duck egg on my head, yes."

"Where did you get that?"

"I fell after you'd gone. But never mind: I'll tell you later."

Samuel Baines grabbed the rope and threw it down again. His task was rendered more or less simple by reason of the glare in which he was working. Had it been dark the rescue effort would have been a very hazardous undertaking indeed.

Gwen was brought safely to the top, and then Bertie. In concern Clara looked at Gwen's swollen ankle.

"I don't like the look at that, Sam," she said worriedly. "A doctor ought to fix her up."

"I agree. Let's be on our way. I'll carry her—and the next time you get a bright idea like this, Bertie, I'll skin you alive! If you'd have done as you were told there wouldn't have been any need for all this."

"Sorry, Dad," Bertie muttered, mooching along in the rear.

The barrier-fence at the end of the pathway proved a sizable barrier, especially with Gwen needing delicate handling, but it was finally mastered. Afterwards it was only a short distance to the cave exit, but as they neared it they began to slow down. They could see perfectly well that, outside, things were very different. The rocks were shining with an uncanny brilliance, just as though they had been swamped with liquid fire.

"Looks mighty hot outside," Samuel Baines muttered, lowering Gwen to her sound foot.

Claire glanced at him. "It is! I found that out earlier on. It was a hundred then, and I'm sure it's hotter now."

"Soon check on it. There's a thermometer along here some-where."

Samuel Baines went off to discover it and Claire and the two children remained hesitating at the cave entrance way. In one sense they were all relieved to have been rescued from the ledge: in another they were filled with a deepening sense of alarm at the fact sunlight was shining through rock and that it was becoming unbearably hot.

"It's a hundred and fifteen," Samuel Baines said, coming back into view. "I never heard of anything like it—especially inside a cave. But then, I never heard of sunlight shining through rock, either. I'm afraid we've got to risk it. Gwen's ankle must be fixed."

"I don't think it needs it, Dad," Gwen said. "It's all right now. See!"

It was quite unbelievable, but there was no denying the fact that the ankle had indeed returned to normal. It was at this moment that Claire also discovered something and her eyes opened wide.

"I've lost my rheumatism!" she exclaimed. "I've had it shocking in my right arm and leg—and now it's gone! I'm—I'm glad, of course, but I'm getting scared. What's suddenly started curing us?"

"Radiations," Samuel Baines said vaguely. He had no idea

how right he was, but in this instance the radiations were filtered in a way very different from those that had lifted Martin Horsley to the heights of perfect happiness.

Within this cave, with many feet of rock intervening, and most of it traced through with layers of tin, copper, lead, and even small scatterings of uranium, the unmasked radiations of the sun were undergoing a deflective process. Light got through, and so did infrared, but cosmic rays were definitely deflected. Others, much shorter and unknown up to now in the spectrum scale, succeeded in penetrating and their effect on human tissue was extraordinary in that they instantly destroyed any untoward condition. Here, if only medical science had had the opportunity to seize and analyse it, was a radiation that was the panacea for all ills. Properly applied, this radiation could have banished cancer and other scourges from the face of the Earth, but, such is the inscrutable way of Fate, it had fallen to a humble man and his family to have their everyday aches and pains cured whilst they gaped at the wonder of it all.

And, apparently, they were alone. What other 'explorers' there had been had evidently made a dash for it before the heat had become excessive.

"Seems to me," Claire said finally, "that the most sensible course for us is to stay in here until this lets up. We'll get sunstroke or something out there."

"More than probable," Samuel Baines agreed, "and we certainly can't catch cold whatever else happens. I just wonder how the rest of the world is faring? This is quite the most amazing day in its history, I should imagine."

Had he been able to see the amazing things that were happening in every part of the planet, Samuel Baines would have realised what an understatement he had made. The buried corners were buried no more; the hidden secrets of the dark no longer existed. Some were dying; some were devolving; others were discovering good health; still others were becoming superbeings for a brief while.

* * * * * * *

And in the Nissen hut at a different point of the Pennines to the Great Peak Cavern, Douglas Taylor and Gordon Briggs both sat stripped to the waist before the radio apparatus. Power still flowed through it and either there was a trick in the fabric of space or else there was some kind of blurred communication trying to make itself apparent.

For over two hours now, whilst they had sat in the blistering heat with the sun shining through the solid roof, the two 'hams' had been concentrating on this mysterious tracery that kept repeating itself amidst the tangle of static caused by the warp in space.

"Can't be anything really," Gordon said finally, always slow to believe anything out of the ordinary. "We're picking up interference from a generating station somewhere."

"Not with this rig." Douglas shook his head firmly. "I have screened it in every possible way and interference just isn't possible. These signals are definitely coming from the outer deeps."

"But how can they be with space so disturbed?"

"As far as I can see it depends upon the degree of disturbance. Light waves and heat waves are still travelling as they always did, the only difference being they've gained in intensity. So I assume that any ultra-short transmission wave may also be taking a direct course, and any interstellar transmission might reach here with greater intensity than any before. Keep an eye on that recording tape—I don't want to lose any of this!"

"No problem—we've several hours left yet." Gordon fell silent, and did not look at all convinced of the value of the exercise. He adjusted the headphones attached to the speaker and concentrated, as well as he could with the distraction of the broiling heat. After a while he asked a question. "Isn't it likely that, because no one could possibly translate an alien language just by listening to it, the creatures behind it might instead broadcast in mathematics—which we believe to be a universal language?"

"Possibly," Douglas admitted, and smiled faintly. "But even then the signals might turn out to be a natural phenomenon, and not artificial. Remember all that kerfuffle years ago when strange signals were received at precisely identical intervals? At first some people thought they were genuine little green men. But they were natural!"

"Yeah—I remember. That's when they discovered pulsars. You think this might be something similar?"

"I'm not sure—but I don't think so."

They fell quiet, listening to the reedy, up-and-down noise, somewhat like an oscillation whistle, superimposed on the midst of the static chaos. Only it was not an oscillation whistle. It was something different, something from away out in space, and both of them knew it. Then suddenly, as they were straining to make sense of it, it blanked out.

Impatiently Douglas reached out to the controls and adjusted them, but all his 'fishing' failed to restore the signal. .

There was only the crackling static and the dancing waves on the oscillograph.

"No use," Douglas grunted, tugging off the headphones and rubbing his ears tenderly. "We've lost it."

Gordon removed his own phones and sat thinking for a moment or two, then he shrugged. "Can't say we didn't try. What do we do now? Give up?"

"I'll never do that! Better leave the speaker and recorder in operation and see if anything else happens. Meantime we'll take a check on what else is happening."

The instruments he had around him were mostly home made, but they were accurate enough, where the warp did not affect them unduly, to reveal that heat waves, light waves, and a fair percentage of cosmic waves were battering through the roof of the Nissen hut. Douglas compressed his lips as he made this discovery and then looked about him.

"As I said earlier," Gordon remarked, "we're in plenty of danger with all these radiations flooding around us. Mystery to me is that they haven't attacked us so far. Apart from this ghastly heat I don't feel any ill effects, though. Do you?"

"No. If we had some lead or something we might be able to rig up a kind of shelter and keep under it. It ought to stop the shorter wavelengths like cosmic."

"By sunset there won't be any more need for protection, will there?"

"On the contrary. Cosmic waves don't emanate from the sun, Gordon. At least not in any great quantity. They come from space itself day and night. Science proved that long ago. But space is evidently in such an agitated state that its normal powers of absorption and deflection are set at zero. It is, though, mighty queer that we haven't been affected in any way."

"Let's hope the luck holds," Gordon murmured, crossing his fingers and holding them up.

What neither of them had realised, chiefly because they were not general scientists but merely enthusiastic radio amateurs, was that the deflective electrical field set up by their apparatus was making it impossible for the incoming radiations to have any direct effect—at least within a fixed radius of the apparatus at which they sat. Beyond it, by the further wall of the hut for instance, the danger was considerable, but they were blissfully unaware of it. The agitation in the region of the transmitter and generator was tremendous, the outflowing force quite sufficient to act as a neutralising screen. The only radiations not affected by this electrical 'spill' were light and heat, but neither of these constituted a vital danger at the moment.

"Have a cigarette," Gordon invited, holding out a squashed packet.

"Thanks." Douglas took one, then he nearly dropped it from his fingers as there came a resumption of the strange signals from the loudspeaker, warped and distorted with distance and static.

Gordon's face was a study for a second or two, his mouth wide open and his eyes fixed in stupefied bewilderment on the loudspeaker. When he wanted to speak he could not: he could only motion with his hand and gulp.

Douglas was the first to recover. He threw down the cigarette and crouched over the apparatus, making sure that everything was still being recorded.

Douglas jammed on his headphones and Gordon did likewise. For the moment nothing else mattered but the extraordinary fact that they seemed to have got a result.

Twenty minutes later the signal ceased. There was only the blur of static in headphones and speaker—nothing more.

For half an hour, then an hour, Douglas and Gordon tested and experimented and sweated, but the communication was completely lost.

"So what happens now?" Gordon asked at last. "We've made a recording and—subject to professional scientists analysing and authenticating it—possibly an amazing discovery concerning extra-terrestrial life. That is, assuming we're going to pull out of this dangerous warp."

"I think we will," Douglas answered quietly. "And what a tale we have to tell when this is all over!"

CHAPTER SIX
UP FROM THE DEPTHS

For the passengers and crew aboard the *Queen Enid* the space warp produced the most incredible creations of all. The seemingly concrete views of first the Sphinx and Pyramids, and then New York City had faded now and instead there were phantom ships seen drifting in many parts of the glassy ocean, most of them appearing to be curiously suspended above the face of the deep and, obviously, merely the creation of diffracted light-waves from another part of the sea.

The temperature on the open deck registered 150 degrees, but, overpowering though it was, most of the passengers hid themselves amidst the superstructure—through which the setting sun none the less shone—and looked out on the ocean in genuine fear. One or two had been stricken down with heat prostration and others with curious mental ailments, but the majority—Dennis Archer and Betty Walford amongst them—were still in possession of their faculties and watching for that blessed moment when the sizzling sun would be masked by the horizon.

Meantime, the liner drifted—and during this time things which Rilson, or his crew and passengers, could never have dreamed of were happening, deep down in the ocean's depths. Here, where light had never penetrated since the world had cooled, blinding brilliance was pouring as the sun's rays shone directly through the earth. It stirred to life monstrous denizens of the deep, blind and gigantic terrors which had never known light, and which struggled away from it frantically as it poured into their subterranean retreat. Upwards towards the surface, in an endeavour to flee from the devouring brilliance, came all manner of maritime life, all of it unclassified in the annals of sea inhabitants.

"What do you make of it, Mr. Denham?" Rilson asked, after he and the first mate had been studying the view from the bridge for a while. "I never saw the ocean so alive before."

"Never been a time before, sir, when the ocean was transparent," the first mate answered. "Look at that infernal thing out there!" He pointed quickly. "If I didn't see it with my own eyes as I do now I'd swear it's a sea-serpent."

He was quite right, though he had something of a seaman's fear of perpetuating a sea myth. This was definitely no myth, however. With succeeding generations of evolution the sea-serpent of the prehistoric had sunk lower and lower into the depths of the ocean, only emerging at intervals through some internal disturbance in .the deeps—but now it had come to the surface with the rest of the giants, a monstrous undulating reptile of quite two hundred feet in length.

Other things were appearing too: gigantic saurian heads, objects like mammoth octopi, and fish with saw beaks powerful enough to rend a small yacht in twain.

"This is getting dangerous," Rilson decided abruptly. "Order all fit men to their posts and have the passengers take a hand too. These infernal things will wreck the ship if we don't deal with them right away."

His order was instantly obeyed and a few minutes later, passengers and crew alike set about the task of defending their lives against the sea monsters bent on destroying them. Not being a war vessel the *Queen Enid* was not very well supplied with armament, but she had one or two guns which succeeded in giving a good account of themselves. An hour later the attack was over and, pursued by the blazing brilliance of the sun shining underneath the sea, the weary passengers floundered below for rest and, if possible, some sanctuary from the glare relentlessly surrounding them.

But for Commander Rilson there was no rest. During the onslaught on the deep sea fish the vessel had drifted to an amazing extent and was now within sight of the Azores Islands.

"Better find some men capable of manning the engine room, sir," Denham said. "If we drift onto those we're liable to stove in."

"True." Rilson's voice sounded abstracted as he gazed into the blazing flood of light at right angles to his line of vision. Then at the first mate's glance of enquiry he added: "I'm just trying to determine what all that is, Mr. Denham. It isn't moving, so it isn't life—but I never saw anything quite so extraordinary."

The Azores Islands were no longer islands as such. Their tops were visible above the thin line that marked the surface of the ocean: after that they became mountainsides, going down into the brilliantly lighted depths. And, at what must have been the level of the ocean floor itself, there lay a city of white stone, overhung in parts by mighty undersea forests.

"Definitely a buried city," Denham said at last.

"That place," Rilson said, "is Atlantis! There can be no doubt of it. Scientists have theorized on its position and placed it on the one-time continent of Mu, which is now the bed of the Atlantic Ocean. And the Azores Islands are the peaks of the mountains around Atlantis. Yes, no doubt of it. Get a camera quickly."

Denham quickly obeyed and within a few minutes the lost city had been recorded for future study. This done Rilson gave the order for all men capable of tolerating the engine room to get below immediately.

* * * * * * *

In Mike Woodcroft's country bungalow the Earth's flight through the flaw in the ether meant mounting anguish as the hours crawled by.

"I could stand this better if it were not far this blasted sun!" Mike panted, after a long silence. "You can't get away from it!

No shelter—no way to stop it! It blazes, an' blazes, an' blazes!" His voice cracked. "There must be some way!"

He lurched uncertainly to his feet, stumbled to the doorway and looked outside stupidly. There were no shadows! Fantastic! Impossible!

"It's killing my eyes," Evelyn groaned, turning her head wearily and flinging an unavailing arm across her face. "It's—it's like looking into a full-powered searchlight a few yards away."

"Be night soon, thank God!" Mike whispered, lurching back into the room and heading once more towards the drinks.

Janet watched his progress and wiped a sodden hand over her lips. "I shouldn't take too much of that, Mike," she warned. "It might do things to you."

"What d'you want me to do, die of thirst?" he demanded.

"It isn't that, Mike, but it is supposed to be dangerous. That's why I'm trying to hold off."

"Mebby I haven't got your will-power," Mike growled, and with that he drank greedily, pure fiery spirit that he did not even trouble to soda down.

With a temperature ranging near 140 degrees you cannot do that and expect to get away with it. After he had finished drinking he stood for a moment or two swaying, slaked for the moment, sweat pouring down his face and bare chest. Then he made an effort to move back to his chair. On his way to it he stopped abruptly and crashed over on his face to the floor.

"The darned idiot!" Evelyn exclaimed, scrambling wearily from her chair. "He's drunk." She tumbled on her knees and dragged heavily at Mike's broad shoulders. Then a new expression came to her face. It was between surprise and unspeakable misery. "Say, he isn't—he isn't drunk—" Her words were hardly audible. "I think he's—dead!"

Janet and Prayerbook hurried over to her side and made a quick examination, but there was nothing they could do.

"Well, don't stand looking at him!" Evelyn shrieked, tears and perspiration coursing together down her cheeks.

"Better put him in the bedroom," Janet said quietly. "And I'm sorry, Evelyn. I know you loved him in a pretty big way."

Evelyn did not answer. She was too stunned with events to make any comment, so Prayerbook made a signal and he and Janet between them heaved the corpse into one of the adjoining bedrooms and dumped it on the bed.

"She's certainly taking it very badly," Prayerbook said, rubbing his pointed chin. He was not showing any sign yet of breaking down himself. He had a cold, hard nature that, so far, not even a cosmic fault had been able to disturb. He peered at Janet for a moment as she stood in front of him. Every bone in her body was outlined against the glare. She was a small, slender skeleton with the vaguest outline of her flesh showing in shimmering waves against the mad light photons.

"Plenty of fires now," she said, looking through the open doorway. "Three more over there! How's the temperature going now?"

"Hundred an' forty-five," Prayerbook answered, squinting at the mercury—then gradually a surprised look came to his face. "Say, it was around that a few minutes ago when Mike passed out."

His voice stopped and Janet could feel the urgency in his manner. "What is it?" she asked, turning sharply and looking at him.

"I—I dunno. But unless I'm crazy this mercury has stopped rising at last! If that's the case the heat isn't getting any worse!"

Janet moved to his side, breathing heavily, brushing the damp strands of hair from her face. To their tortured vision the thermometer hung in a haze of brilliance, the sun blazing through the wooden wall as it hung low over the horizon.

A minute passed, two minutes, but the mercury remained steady, practically at the limit of its column expansion. Janet and Prayerbook did not know it any more than anybody else in the world, but the distorted heat radiation that had enveloped Earth had reached the maximum. The highest recorded temperature was proved afterwards to have been at Barbados, where an all-time high of 182 degrees Fahrenheit in the interior of buildings was reached.

Prayerbook turned away at last, frowning. He gave a glance about him and then looked enquiry at Janet.

"Wonder what Evelyn's doing? She's mighty quiet. I'd better take a look. Struck me, as it did you, that her mind isn't any too steady."

He crossed to the bedroom and peeped inside. Evelyn was lying on her back beside the dead body of Mike, her hands locked behind her blonde head. From the gentle heaving of her breast it looked as though she had at last found relief in sleep.

"Asleep—beside him," Prayerbook muttered, coming back to Janet. "Seems sort of gruesome to me. The dead are dead. I say. Nothing you can do about that."

He rubbed his sore, light-blurred eyes and sat down beside the table again. Janet moistened her lips with a drop or two of soda water—nothing more. It tasted flat and warm. Then she came and sat at Prayerbook's side. "Be sunset soon," she whispered.

"Uh-huh. 'Bout time, too!"

Like countless millions of others in the world they waited for that moment when the appalling sun would dip below the horizon—just as, like the others, they did not comprehend how complete was the disorder in light-waves. The truth only came to them when, after touching the horizon, the sun did not set, but blazed with the same relentless fury as before.

At first neither Janet nor Prayerbook could believe it. They suspected some tremendous refraction in the atmosphere that was making the sun appear to linger whereas is actually must be below the horizon—then, very slowly, it dawned on them what had happened. Earth appeared, as it had to everybody else, to be made of glass. The sun sank lower until it was casting its rays obliquely. To look down towards the sun was horrifying; dizzying, and an even greater shock because relief had been expected. Instead terror was added to terror.

"It can't be!" Janet cried, beating her fist on the table. "No!

The sun can't shine through the ground like this! We've got delusions or something."

"Perhaps it's the end of the world," Prayerbook whispered. "It says in the Bible—'And the heavens shall pass away with a great noise and the elements shall melt with fervent heat; the earth also and the works that are therein shall be burned up.' Jan, there's no night any more! No night! It's an endless day!"

For the first time there was a crack in the steel-hard armour of a killer; the first real trace of fear in the make-up of a man who spouted Scriptures whilst he watched a victim die slowly.

"Take is easy," Janet muttered, her face drawn. "Don't go off the deep end, Prayerbook. That isn't your way."

She watched him intently, her eyes aching. He gave her a blank kind of look. "No night," he repeated huskily, flinging up useless arms over his face to hide the glare. "I can't stand it, Jan! I've got to get away from it! Hide myself! I've got to! Don't you understand?"

Suddenly he leapt to his feet, plunged past the girl, and then ran like a madman down the shale driveway outside. Janet tried to follow his movements but the oblique-angled sun was blazing up at her in a sea of unholy flame. She called once—weakly, despairingly.

"Prayerbook, come back here! Come back!"

But he did not come back. He did not attempt to drive the car—in any case it would have seared the skin from his hands had he even tried. In fact he did not attempt anything normal. He was motivated by one desire only, to find darkness and rest in a world from which night had been stripped. Perhaps he blundered into one of the grass fires, perhaps he devolved into some grotesque primordial strain, perhaps a lot of things. In the records of people missing after the Endless Day his name never appeared.

Janet turned slowly, stunned with the realization that she was now alone with one emotionally overwrought woman and a dead man. She pressed a hand to her throbbing forehead and stood for a while with her back to the sunlight. It gave her some relief but its heat was sickening in the extreme.

Wearily she crawled across to the thermometer and looked at it. It registered 143 degrees. It had dropped by two. Janet's cracked lips parted in a smile of thankfulness for a moment.

Slowly, as she looked about her, Janet realized that she was struggling with impossible things. She had got to get help somehow. The thought of police did not worry her now. She would be roped in with Evelyn, of course, as an accessory, but her own conscience was clear. Evelyn was the killer, the one who had reason to be afraid.

Get out! Get back to London somehow! That was the answer. Janet swung round dizzily and headed for the bedroom door. Behind her, somewhere beneath her feet, a liquid circle of intolerable flame was burning. It gave her the light-headed impression of walking in space or across a floor of perfectly clear glass.

Janet entered the bedroom silently and Evelyn stirred a little and seemed to be listening for something. Then she squirmed up on the bed where the dead Mike lay beside her. She drew her slender bare legs over the bed edge and planted her feet on the floor.

"Oh, it's you, Jan—" For some reason there was half a question in her voice.

"Yes." Janet was glad Evelyn was more rational. Her fit of emotion seemed to have passed. "I—I couldn't stick it out there in the living room. It's terrifying when you're trying to face it alone."

"Are you trying to tell me? You've got Prayerbook, haven't you? As much as the louse is worth, anyway."

Janet did not answer. For some reason she wanted to cry, but she didn't.

"Is—is it night, or day, or what?" Evelyn mumbled, and Janet, preoccupied, missed a certain significance in the question.

"It's—it's both." Janet paused for a moment at her own unusual statement. "The sun hasn't set, Eve, as you can see for yourself. It's shining right through the ground!"

"So that's it!" Evelyn rubbed impatient hands through her

thick blonde hair. "Whoever heard of a sun shining at night? The world's coming to an end, that's what it is—just as Prayerbook said. Maybe there's something in his psalm-smiting ideas after all. Sort of see the future, eh?"

"Maybe," Janet whispered, and Evelyn gave her a curiously vacant look.

"What are you so damned quiet about? Can't be the sun still getting you down, surely? You ought to have got used to it by now."

"It's not that, Evelyn. It's Prayerbook. He's—he's gone."

"Gone where?"

"I don't know. He broke down and just dashed outside. I shouted after him but he didn't come back. He never will now. I know that. I know he was tough, hard as rock, but he was something to swing onto. I feel so desperately lost without him."

"Hard lines, kid. I'm sorry for you. I suppose he was your man after all—same as Mike was mine. Looks like the woman always pays, eh?"

Janet went over to the bed and sat down beside the other girl, putting an arm about her shoulders.

"Evelyn, we've got to get out and risk it. We just can't stay here. We might stand a chance back in London. I'll drive the car."

"Don't be an idiot!" Evelyn replied flatly. "That car must be that flaming hot it'd rip the skin from you if you tried it. Anyway, of you could get as far as starting the engine you'd probably have it burst into flames. Can't take a risk like that. Anyway, what good would it do us to go back to London? We'd only be picked up."

"What does that matter? Be better than this, anyway!"

Evelyn moved a languid arm. "You go on, kid, and run back to the city and the police. They won't do much to you anyway: you're too nice. But I'm stopping!"

Janet made no movement there and then. Evelyn hesitated as if making up her mind over something, then she got to her feet and staggered uncertainly from the bedroom into the living room, clutching tenaciously at the wall as she went. Janet watched her for a moment and then silently followed. At an angle beneath them, pouring up out of the void, was the unmasked and terrifying glare.

"I—I tried to sleep in that room," Evelyn said, fumbling for a glass so clumsily that Janet helped her and placed it, with a small quantity of soda water in it, in her hand. "I couldn't get away from the light, Jan. It soaked through me, through my eyelids. I tried everything. I think I fell asleep at last, worn out. I fell asleep looking at that hell-fired sun. Bit queer, eh? I never heard of anybody doing that outside maybe a Hindu ascetic."

Evelyn gulped down the soda water, made a wry face, then shrugged her smooth, undraped shoulders. She was completely naked save for the decencies. "Doesn't seem quite so hot as it was," she commented, giving a dull look around her.

"It isn't. The temperature dropped two degrees not so long ago. I haven't looked since—but I will." Janet hurried over to the thermometer and studied it. Her heart beat a little faster with relief. It had climbed down to 139 degrees.

"Well?" Evelyn asked her. "Any cooler?"

"Definitely. Five degrees lower than it was and still slowly dropping. I think we re through the worst—unless it comes back."

"Wouldn't be surprised," Evelyn growled. Then after a moment or two's silence she added, "Well, go on, Jan. Since it's a shade cooler maybe you can snatch safety. Don't bother about me. I'll stay and fry if the fires catch up. If they don't—well, who cares anyway?"

Janet was silent, debating the situation. Evelyn waited for a moment—then suddenly all her struggle for calmness broke down. She laughed desperately, the safety valve of emotion too long pent. The steaming silence rang with it. Janet seized her and forced her across the blazing abyss to a chair, nearly flinging her into it.

"Evelyn, stop it! Stop it!" Janet landed a stinging slap across the face. "Stop behaving like a child! Let's get out of here—

both of us! Grab some clothes and we'll go."

"No!" Evelyn shook her head stubbornly in between gusts of laughter. "I'm not going anywhere. I told you that—and I meant it!"

"Evelyn, stop talking like an idiot! We just can't stay here—"

Janet stopped dead, conscious of the incredible. She waited, breathing hard, every nerve tautened to breaking point. She did not dare believe what she saw. The glare beneath her feet, that flaming brilliance ninety-three-million miles away, was dimming! Very slowly the effulgence was fading!

She blinked and rubbed her eyes, fearful for the moment that they were failing after the punishment they had endured. Finally she stumbled across to the cigarette lighter on the table by the open window. Striking the flint she gazed at the resultant steady flame. It was perfectly normal and bright. Nothing wrong with her sight then.

She waited again with a palpitating heart. The mad sun was smothering itself in seas of dark infinity beneath her feet. She could at last look upon it without hurt, see it fading into a red ball. Everybody on the "night" hemisphere was looking at it at that moment, aware that the hellish adventure with mad light-waves was at an end. Earth was swimming gradually free of the warp in space and normal laws were commencing to reassert themselves.

The last spark faded out of the underground sun. Black! The floor solid as it had always been. Outside—the blessed night.

Janet sucked in a deep breath and felt her eyes twitching as restful, normal darkness surrounded her. Picking up the cigarette lighter again she flicked it into flame in front of the thermometer. The mercury had dropped to 120 degrees. Heat radiation was reverting to normal as the last edges of the warp were crossed and Earth sailed out into normal space.

"Well, are you going or not?" Evelyn demanded from the gloom.

Janet gave a start and then frowned. The question was odd considering the enormity of the blessed thing that had just happened. "We're both going now," she said.

"Why now? My decision hasn't changed a jot, Jan. I'm not going because of a glare—"

"The glare's gone, Evelyn. The hell is over."

There was silence—then a low, choked laugh out of the night. "And I thought I'd fooled you, Jan! You little idiot! Don't you see why I want to stay here and rot—or fry? With Mike in there, I'm no good any more! I'm stone blind! I fell asleep staring at the sun through my eyelids. I did it purposely! I said I wanted peace, and dark, and I got it! Well, maybe I deserve this. I'm finished, kid. You get out. You're decent, and always were—"

Janet said nothing. Somehow she had half guessed it. The odd question Evelyn had asked: the way she had fumbled her drink—but she had to be taken away. She would be taken away—by force if need be. Janet was quite determined on that. "I'm going to get help," she said, and turned to the doorway.

Here she paused for a moment, the quiet of the cooling bungalow disturbed only by Evelyn's bitter sobbing. From far away lightning flashed over the grass fires and there came a menacing rumble of thunder as cool air surged into the ebbing blanket of heat that had tortured the world.

ABOUT THE AUTHOR

British writer JOHN RUSSELL FEARN was born near Manchester, England, in 1908. As a child he devoured the science fiction of Wells and Verne, and was a voracious reader of the Boys' Story Papers. He was also fascinated by the cinema, and first broke into print in 1931 with a series of articles in *Film Weekly*.

He then quickly sold his first novel, *The Intelligence Gigantic*, to the American magazine, *Amazing Stories*. Over the next fifteen years, writing under several pseudonyms, Fearn became one of the most prolific contributors to all of the leading US science fiction pulps, including such legendary publications as *Astounding Stories*, *Startling Stories*, *Thrilling Wonder Stories*, and *Weird Tales*.

During the late 1940s he diversified into writing novels for the UK market, and also created his famous superwoman character, The Golden Amazon, for the prestigious Canadian magazine, the Toronto *Star Weekly*. In the early 1950s in the UK, his fifty-two novels as "Vargo Statten" were bestsellers, most notably his novelization of the film, *Creature from the Black Lagoon*.

Apart from science fiction, he had equal success with westerns, romances, and detective fiction, writing an amazing total of 180 novels—most of them in a period of just ten years—before his early death in 1960. His work has been translated into nine languages, and continues to be reprinted and read worldwide.

www.ingramcontent.com/pod-product-compliance
Lightning Source LLC
Chambersburg PA
CBHW050752250626
47155CB00005B/2030

Borgo Press Books by JOHN RUSSELL FEARN

1,000-Year Voyage: A Science Fiction Novel
The Crimson Rambler: A Crime Novel
Don't Touch Me: A Crime Novel
The Empty Coffins: A Mystery of Horror
The Fourth Door: A Mystery Novel
From Afar: A Science Fiction Mystery
The G-Bomb: A Science Fiction Novel
Here and Now: A Science Fiction Novel
Into the Unknown: A Science Fiction Tale
The Man Who Was Not: A Crime Novel
One Way Out: A Crime Novel (with Philip Harbottle)
Shattering Glass: A Crime Novel
Slaves of Ijax: A Science Fiction Novel
The Space Warp: A Science Fiction Novel
What Happened to Hammond? A Scientific Mystery

INTO THE
UNKNOWN

A SCIENCE FICTION TALE

JOHN RUSSELL FEARN

THE BORGO PRESS

MMXII

INTO THE UNKNOWN

FIRST BORGO PRESS EDITION

Published by Wildside Press LLC

www.wildsidebooks.com

DEDICATION

For Arthur Philip King

CONTENTS

INTO THE UNKNOWN
A SCIENCE FICTION TALE

THE Omnipotent Observer paused in his cosmic journey to study a change that had come to the Earthly solar system. To him, it all occurred in one split second of infinite Time—but that reversion, that retreat, was so enormous and colossal that even he was interested—interested enough to record the whole outstanding event within his limitless mind. A literal defiance of Time itself was indeed something worth pausing for.

He watched, and beheld....

* * * * * * *

WITHIN the home of Doctor Cassell Thurman, physicist, reigned the joyous abandon of a New Year party. What was more, it was also the first marriage anniversary of his daughter Ann, and Rodney Shenstone.

"It surprises me, Doc, that a savant like yourself should be able to enjoy a party," Shenstone commented, during an interval in the almost continuous round of drinks and rising merriment. "You disprove all the old theories about scientists being cold-blooded."

Thurman smiled faintly, tossing aside on the mantle-shelf a small chamois-leather bag, which he had been absently examining.

"Scientists are as human as anybody else," he answered in his grave voice; then, as his eyes rested on his daughter's

slender figure amidst the guests, his voice took on a new animation. "Besides, I'd do anything for Ann, Rodney.... Anything!"

"And I," her husband added, slightly uncomfortable. Thurman had been a widower for the past seven years. "Still, for all that, I can't help but feel you've got a double motive in throwing this party. I mean, despite it being our anniversary and New Year's Eve—"

"Yes, I have a motive," Thurman assented, dropping his voice somewhat as the radio dance music ceased for an instant. "At five minutes to midnight I'm going to show you all my latest invention."

Rodney evinced little surprise. As a Research scientist working for the Government, Thurman's reputation in atomic physics had been unmatched. Although he had officially retired some years ago, he still continued his own private research. That he had been working on an especial 'something' Rodney knew full well, as his son-in-law.

"Yes, tonight is an ideal occasion to reveal the secrets of Time," Thurman continued cryptically. "Being New Year's Eve, I mean."

"Time?" Rodney's own radio-engineering instincts were aroused. A blond, slightly chubby young man, he had a much higher intellectual quota than one would have imagined. As resident maintenance engineer with the World Broadcasting Corporation he could not afford to be a fool. "Don't tell me it's the fourth dimension!" he chuckled. The older man shook his head.

"No, my boy—anything but it. Besides, this isn't a time-traveling system; that's out of the question. It's something else, which postulates the possibilities lying in space itself. It ought to—we'll discuss it later. Here's Ann."

The girl herself, ash-blonde and twenty-four, came forward with an impish tread. Her wide gray eyes were sparkling mischievously. She patted her father affectionately on the summit of his nearly-bald cranium.

"Dad, it's twenty minutes to midnight," she said, apparently

with some effort. It was more than obvious that she had not abstained from drinking liqueurs and cocktails. "You promised me something at five to twelve. What is it? Another present?"

"My dear Ann, you've had your present," the Doctor reminded her, indicating her gold wristwatch. "Besides, what do you expect for one year only? Keep it up for twenty years, and maybe I'll leave you my fortune. No, it's not a second present," he continued, coming down to the issue. "It is the—er—preview of my invention. An invention with immense possibilities. It's in the laboratory across the way. As you and Rod know, I've been working in secret for some years now."

Ann wrinkled her nose in disfavor. "Do we have to go into that smelly old place?" she complained. "I don't like the things you have lying about." She paused, then her gray eyes opening wider in purely girlish curiosity she asked, "What have you got tucked away in there anyway? You've never told anybody anything."

Thurman chuckled good-naturedly. "I will soon enough. I'll be handing over full details to government experts. But meanwhile—" he raised his hand for quiet. The radio and record player were respectfully silenced and the guests ceased talking.

"My friends, you're going to behold something extraordinary," he announced. "Follow me into my laboratory.... There will be a demonstration shortly at five to twelve."

He moved to the interconnecting door of the immense drawing room and flung it open. The guests followed interestedly— some chanting close-harmony, others a trifle more serious—but certainly all of them were un-inclined for anything particularly erudite. Ann herself was none too precise in her gait; she felt unaccountably heady and prompted towards titters of laughter for no apparent reason. She felt glad of Rodney's hand at her elbow; it did at least save things from walking into her.

Entering the laboratory, Thurman switched on the light and in silence, motioned the guests around him. He stood gazing with fond pride upon a truly massive machine supported on pillars of solid concrete, perhaps a couple of feet from the floor.

In some aspects the gigantic instrument—from floor to ceiling almost—resembled an ultra-technical television transmitter, except that at one end it was mainly square in shape, and apparently encased in lead. At one side was a control board of sorts, and an impressive array of switches and buttons. Most incredible of all was an utterly incongruous potted plant flourishing below a lensed projection near the center of the machine.

"What is it?" ventured Bertie Vincent, with his habitual nervous giggle, holding his wineglass at a forty-five-degree angle, regardless of its contents.

"In one way it is a Time-machine," said Thurman. "Time itself, I have proven, is an impossible condition in which to travel by the medium of the Time-machine of popular fiction. But it *is* possible to alter the nature of Time itself."

"Nature of Time?" repeated Ann, swaying gently on her toes. "What's that?"

"Time is in the form of an ever-flowing sea—a sea filling all space, in which our Earth, the solar system, and the rest of the universe, has floated for countless aeons. As the Earth, and all other bodies pass through it, this Time Stream, as one might call it, causes the process we know as progress. A series of events, in which everything passes through a state of Change, and no action can ever repeat itself. All actions, events, represent the *progress* of the objects—or people—involved. And the medium for progress is Time.

"But, by sending into this limitless sea an opposing force it is possible to send this Time-sea flowing backwards, much the same as strong wind will dispel a fog and cause it to retreat over the place where it was formerly progressing."

"What would happen to human beings in this process?" Rodney asked.

"Nothing happens to thinking organisms—at least not in the short intervals I propose using. The human being is something unique in the nature of the universe in that we possess Free Will. Whilst we are caught up in the universal Time-stream we do not 'travel' in the same way as inanimate objects. Of

course—" Thurman broke off, suddenly conscious of an under-current of murmuring and coughing in the small assembly. It was clear that few—if any—of them had the slightest idea what he was talking about. He looked appealingly at Rodney in the awkward silence.

"You mean," Rodney said slowly, "that your machine can make everything other than intelligent life go backwards? Like trees and plants—?" he broke off in astonishment, turning to regard the potted plant in the midst of the apparatus. At first, he had thought it must have been left there by mistake.

"Exactly. Now, if you are ready, I'll give you a brief demon-stration...." Thurman had evidently decided that action was much more preferable to exposition. He paused as he caught sight of Bertie Vincent jabbing a wavering finger towards the machine.

"I want to know what good it is," Vincent asked. "You say it doesn't affect us physically. By that, I suppose you mean we'll see fragments of the past without going there?"

"Correct." Thurman's voice was calm, although his lips were compressed.

"Well, it isn't as though we could view the future! *That* would be worth having! But as it is I see no value in the thing at all," he concluded, with solemn decision.

"A person like you wouldn't, Bertie," Thurman returned dryly. "The precise value of the machine lies in its ability to discover geological data and have it properly tabulated. Past earthly formations can be checked by experts. Of course, crea-tures that have lived and died will no longer be visible, within the scope of the forces I propose using...."

"Now, I want you to watch that potted plant." Thurman moved to his control board, and began to activate switches. There was a faint hum from his apparatus, but that was all.

"Can I help?" Ann asked, then as her father did not appear to hear her she disengaged her arm from Rodney's steadying hand, and moved rather rockily forward.

"It's a funny looking thing, isn't it?" she went on, with a giggle. Thurman ignored her, intent on his work.

"All of you—look at the plant!" he snapped, turning away from the switchboard. Ann turned too, frowning, but remained where she was.

A peculiar thing was happening to the plant. It seemed to be waving in an invisible breeze, then gradually it began to shrink. The leaves and blossom disappeared into thin shoots, like blades of grass. For a moment a single green shoot peeped above the soil—which did not seem to be affected unduly—and then abruptly it disappeared.

"Where—where did it go to?" Bertie's voice rose unsteadily.

Before Thurman could answer, Ann's voice came from beside the switchboard. "Don't worry, Bertie. I saw which switch Dad pressed to start it. I'll bring it back for you." She giggled, and reeled unsteadily forward. Her fingers settled on a prominent blue switch.

Thurman started violently as he beheld the position of his daughter's hand.

"Ann!" he shouted hoarsely, leaping forward. "Get away, you little fool!"

He clutched her arm desperately, but his very action precipitated what he was striving to avoid. Ann staggered, but did not relax her grip on the switch. She snapped it clean over in its slot.

Instantly things began to happen. The muted hum of the machine changed to a deafening scream, which cut off dead almost immediately. In that same moment, the needles upon the dials affixed to the main switchboard flickered over to zero and stopped. A few seconds later the lights went out. A faint light remained, sufficient to see adequately for perhaps ten feet. It came from the skylight above.

The onlookers in the front gasped. The plant pot had completely disappeared even as they watched.

Ann, slightly sobered, staggered free of her father's grip. Rodney, coming forward, clutched her tightly.

"What's happened, Dad?" she asked blankly. "Have I done

something wrong?"

Thurman did not answer. He merely looked at her.

"Why are you looking at me like that? Why—?"

An incredible expression had settled on Thurman's seamed face. It was something akin to loathing and disgust. He seemed to have aged, and for a moment a light of madness danced in his eyes. He took a step forward towards Ann. Immediately Rodney barred his way.

"Now take it easy, Doctor. Ann didn't—" he broke off uncertainly as Thurman suddenly buried his face in his hands.

"Ann, oh Ann, why on earth did you have to do that?" Then, pulling himself together, Thurman turned to the assembly of guests amidst the gloom of the big laboratory.

"I want you all to try and keep calm whilst I tell you something. First, come back into the drawing room." Somewhat unnerved, the guests filed back through the open doorway into the light and warmth—then, fear getting the better of sense, Bertie Vincent made a dash for the door.

"Let's get out of here! Something horrible has happened—I know it has!"

He made to seize the door handle, then fell back with a yelp of alarm. Round-eyed, he looked back at the others. "I can't touch it!" he breathed hoarsely. "Come on, somebody, and give me a hand."

"Come back here, Bertie, and calm down," ordered Thurman steadily. There was an odd note of command in his voice. "We've got to face this thing squarely—"

"Father!" Ann exclaimed, gazing fixedly at her wrist. "Father! My watch is going *backwards*. My brand new gold watch."

Thurman went over to the girl's side. For quite a minute he stood motionless, his eyes fixed on the bright new dial. Then, as he traced the slow but perceptible backward crawl of the hour hand, he swung round to the others.

"Look at your watches!" he requested curtly. "There's something happening now that substantiates my worst fears beyond all doubt, I'm afraid. Keep a steady eye on your watches, then

tell me what you find."

Hardly daring to imagine what they would behold, the others obeyed—or rather tried to obey. For some curious reason those men owning pocket watches found it impossible to drag them from their pockets. Those owning wristwatches were equally baffled. Beyond question every watch was going backwards.

"Yes, backwards," Thurman told them. He looked round at the room clock. "It was five to twelve when we entered the laboratory. Now it is twenty-five to—"

"Doc, don't just stand there talking like that!" Bertie shouted hysterically. "Tell us what has really happened!"

"I have made a fatal mistake," Thurman answered, a slight tremor in his voice. "To reverse the flow of Time requires tremendous power. My machine, with its self-contained atomic power unit, has that power. But, to operate at all, the energies used must be transmitted at full strength. The outflowing radiations from my machine are capable of transmitting themselves clear across the solar system—"

"But—but the demonstration," Rodney faltered. "That was to encompass only that potted plant beside the machine, wasn't it?"

"That's correct, Rod. And that was my fatal mistake," Thurman said thickly. "My machine also threw out a force-field, a containing web of force that limited the Time-reversing radiations to a small area. Before activating those radiations I threw the switch that set up the force field."

Rodney's brain was racing. "So when Ann reversed the switch she had seen you operate initially, it was *not* the switch that started the machine proper, but the force field? She—*she switched it off!*" he whispered, a note of horror in his voice. He put his arm about his wife's shoulders, as Ann buried her face in his chest.

There was a stunned silence.

"Don't you understand, all of you?" Thurman appealed. "The full power of the machine enveloped the whole laboratory—the city—the whole Earth. Then, out into space. It happened almost

instantly, at the speed of light.

"I should have built in additional safeguards to the machine," Thurman added, as Ann looked up at him, remorse and self-guilt seared across her face. "Made the force-field automatic."

"Why can't you do something about it?" Bertie yelled. "Undo the damage somehow?"

Thurman looked at him disgustedly. "Because," he said deliberately, "the moment the force field shut off, what was present time in the laboratory immediately became *past* time! I cannot touch or affect the machine in any way. Hence the reason why we saw the dials registering zero; the machine had regressed to the time before I switched it on. Similarly with our watches. And that's why you couldn't open the door. It just wasn't open at that instant in past time, same as some watches were inside pockets. Time has placed between us and material things a thin curtain of unbreakable vibration. We can't open doors, we can't even handle our clothes. Nothing can happen to objects save that which has already happened."

"And what about us? What about human beings?" Rodney questioned.

"So far anything that is organic—a thinking creature—is not affected. To do so required a higher order of vibration than my machine was set to. There are many reasons for this, such as Free Will—a thinking being can transfer itself from place to place of its own volition. Inanimate objects can progress only due to natural forces—" he broke off impatiently.

"All this is purely academic, anyhow. In any case, there's no guarantee but what as the Time reversal gathers momentum, human beings may not be caught up in it as well."

"Then how do we get out of here?" someone demanded fiercely.

Thurman looked at him. "When the time comes again that the door was last opened—about 9:30, I think it was—it will open of its own accord. We can then get through the doorway. Meanwhile, the Time reversal will continue. There is no means of checking it, of building a machine to neutralize the effect, as

is theoretically possible. To do that would mean progress, the handling of machinery. It just can't be done. My machine, and Ann's foolhardy action, has changed the entire course of Time."

"But light from the fire; electric light—sound.... All seem to be normal," Rodney muttered, thinking hard.

The physicist shrugged. "Light waves from the fire are reversed. We're getting past impressions. Sound from human voices, from all *living* creatures, will be normal. Our vocal chords are operating in the present. But ordinary sounds will be in reverse."

"And electric light? I can't get the hang of that at all."

"I agree that seems paradoxical," Thurman answered. "We are having light because it existed at this time before, but actually power-houses are creating it in a past time. Those power-house generators will be untouchable. Yet they'll keep going unaided, because they're merely repeating what they've already done." Thurman was becoming visibly weary; he passed a hand across his eyes, then sank down heavily into a nearby armchair.

Instantly he noticed that he was not actually touching it. He was separated from it by perhaps an inch of invisible vibration. The springs did not depress, nor did his agitated, pounding hands leave any dents in the chair's upholstery. Indeed, within the whole room nobody's feet really touched the carpet; again there was that invisible separation.

Thurman rose in exasperation. "When the doors in the house open, you must all go to your homes. Try and keep calm. In the daylight I will attempt to study out the difficulties that beset us.... You, Ann, should go upstairs to your old room and try to sleep." He looked into her haggard eyes. "I'm afraid you need it! You, Rod, will please stay here and talk with me. As an engineer you might find it possible to assist me."

"Fair enough," Rodney responded, then drew the now faintly sobbing Ann to him.

The silence of the dead fell on the dazed assembly. A few of the guests were dumbfoundedly aware that their glasses had mysteriously left their hands. They were now back on the side-

board, spirited away by an invisible agency. And they were dry and clean, whereas not moments before they had been filled nearly to the brim!

Those in Thurman's New York residence could hardly have been expected to perceive the sudden and remarkable things that had happened in the outside world when Time halted in its onward progress.

Instantly everything inanimate ceased to progress. Every living creature could conceive the future, but was baulked in the effort to make that future possible.

Beyond doubt, Ann Shenstone's hand had ended Time. Every clock on Earth was going backwards. The oceans that had been at flood tide suddenly started to ebb before reaching high-water mark, going back over the order they had just covered and leaving *dry* sand behind them!

Every vehicle in the world stopped almost instantly, hurling many people headlong through space ahead of the vehicle, which then pursued a backward course of reverse motion. Thousands were killed outright.

For a second the world was plunged into infinite darkness. The moon and stars vanished; the heavens became an inky vault—then light resumed, bringing with it an astounding revelation.

In America, where the moon had just been rising, it was now going back into the east again. The entire solar system was in reverse.

Every living soul was dumbfounded with amazement and horror at the things that had come to pass. Fortunately humans were unaffected in themselves, and the vast majority of people were alive to witness the chaos around them.

There was a singular case in Sydney where workmen were dynamiting a defunct grain warehouse. They had depressed the explosive switch and seen the entire battered edifice smash into a thousand pieces. Then the end of Time hit them.... They actually saw the lever on the explosive-switch shoot back into position, heard the sound of the explosion in reverse. Most amazing

of all was the sight of the warehouse back exactly as it was to commence with, having risen to its former condition from the shattered debris. The workmen doubted their sanity and promptly went on strike.

All over the world, other shiftings were taking place, but back in New York, Doctor Thurman and Rodney knew nothing of the happenings. Once the doors had opened, the guests had left hurriedly. They departed into quiet and curiously deserted streets, treading on ground that was not ground at all but something invisibly solid. Ann, shaken by the knowledge that she was indirectly responsible for everything, went upstairs to the room she had occupied before her marriage. After an interval the bedroom door opened, and she passed inside. The door shut relentlessly behind her.

Downstairs, Rodney and Thurman talked ceaselessly—all to no avail.

"We can do absolutely nothing!" Thurman declared finally. "Progress has ceased. For a little while we shall be able to eat foodstuffs, because being organic—although dead—they are unaffected by the reversal. But we shall have to eat them before they vanish to the place we got them from. If we eat them first we'll stop that, naturally. Thank God inorganic things alone are affected!"

"Fortunately we've chicken, turkey—all sorts of good things on hand for the festive season," Rodney reflected. "How about drinking though? That's a point."

Thurman nodded. "It certainly is. I've just been thinking it over. Everything is quite untouchable—including water. Milk is the only substitute, coming from an organic creature. I've some skin gourds up in the lumber room which will be similarly unaffected. We'll have to get the milk into those. They're pretty clean, as it happens. I used them once on an exploration trip. The milk may go sour, of course, but we can't pick and choose."

"Going to be darned difficult," Rodney remarked. "As I see it, the very bottles in which the milk is standing will be untouchable, even though the actual milk isn't. Besides, the bottles will

go back finally to where they came from."

"We can take care of that," Thurman answered thoughtfully, picking up the chamois-leather bag with which he had been idly toying earlier in the evening.

"This is my watch-pouch. I'd just had it cleaned, but since I can't get at my watch in my pocket, it's useless for that purpose any longer."

"What's that got to do with milk?" Rodney asked, a trifle testily.

"Isn't it obvious, Rod? This pouch is skin from the chamois, the European antelope. We can use it as a ladle. Slow work, but very necessary. The moment this door here opens again we'll get those gourds from the box-room. Meantime we might go into the laboratory. I'd like to see how things are going on in there."

As they turned towards the connecting door the electric light switch turned itself to 'Off', and the window blinds shot up.

"Good God, it's—it's yesterday afternoon!" Thurman exclaimed, swinging round. "See there—the sun is *rising* in the west!"

Somewhat dazed, the two men passed into the laboratory as the connecting door suddenly opened.

Thurman stood in contemplative silence before the Time-reverser, then he pointed. "See there—the rivets are disappearing." He indicated the terminals from which the nuts were visibly vanishing with every passing moment, leaving loose ends of wire that also began to become non-existent as the minutes passed.

Struck by a sudden thought he went across to a divided tray on the bench and peered amongst the in-numerable odds and ends.

"They're here—where I took them from," he remarked, smiling faintly.

"All reversed time," Thurman continued. "I put those bolts on at exactly this time yesterday. That time has now returned, hence the bolts have returned to their original place. They *had*

to, otherwise they'd be in two places at once."

"But, damn it, nobody touched them! You carried them there in the first place, surely?"

"How they've returned is nothing to do with it," Thurman said firmly. "Things simply cease to be in one place when the time has expired and return to the previous spot."

Rodney stood digesting the paradox in silence for a while. Then he swung round and seized Thurman's arm tightly. "Doc, we can't stand about here like a couple of fools! We've got to do something!"

Thurman shrugged. "How?" he asked, in an empty voice. "Between us and the world we understand is the complex dimension between past and present. Everything about us is apart from us, like a slowly changing dream—yet real, alive, and terrible."

"Hell! No drinks or cigarettes," Rodney said blankly, suddenly recalling personal indulgences. Then, "See here Doctor. How come the radiations from your machine are still existent?"

"Simple. The radiations never existed this time yesterday—have never existed before. That is why they exist now—and will exist—right into past time, because to them it is their only existence. You follow?"

"Hmm, I suppose you're right." Rodney did not look too convinced.

"All this, because Ann had too much to drink last night," Thurman added, frowning.

Rodney looked at him steadily. "You can't blame her, Doc. She was only having a good time, like the rest of us. You should never have made your infernal machine in the first place."

Thurman sighed and turned heavy eyes to the slowly vanishing machine.

"Probably you're right.... Well, I'm going to try and get into that box-room. Once we've done that milk job I'll get a little sleep—you too, Rod. You need it. When we're refreshed we'll see how we can face up to things. How to live in a world without progress...."

The milk transference finally accomplished, Rodney waited for the bedroom door to open. He found his wife fully dressed and obviously very much alarmed, sitting in the center of a neatly made bed. There was no sign of depression from the weight of her body.

"Oh, Rod, I've been so scared! Things keep happening by magic. When I came up here to go to bed I couldn't get my clothes off. My hands seemed to go through them instead of holding them. I tried to get my watch off and couldn't—" she broke off as Rodney came forward and took her hand. Suddenly he frowned.

"Your watch? It's gone. I thought you said—"

"That's *it*!" Ann cried agitatedly. "It just disappeared whilst I was looking at it. Then I tried to get into the bed, but my hands seemed to go through the bedclothes. I lay on top of them for a while. I guess I must have slept for a while. But when I woke up I was dressed in this morning frock, instead of my evening dress! Rod, what's happening?"

Rodney hugged her affectionately.

"It does seem weird," he agreed. "Matter of fact, it's now yesterday! That's why you couldn't get your things off—they were *on* at that time yesterday evening, at the party. The bed too would be made at a different time again, and couldn't be altered. Then your clothes changed of their own accord whilst you slept, because yesterday at this time you had that dress on. That time has come round again now. You see?"

The girl shook her head vehemently. "No! I don't see! Why do these things happen? How is it your clothes haven't changed?"

Rodney shrugged. "Purely because I had this suit on all day yesterday and all night. Suddenly, I expect, I'll find myself in pyjamas," he grinned cynically. "It's a terrible mess," he went on more seriously. "Who knows what's going to happen as things go on?"

"And I did it," the girl muttered, staring through the window. "I did it. I was crazy last night, Rod; had too much to drink. Why on earth didn't you stop me? You know what a fool I am

when I get too much to drink—"

"Forget it," Rodney snapped. "I guess we were *all* crazy last night—your father more so than anybody with his damned machine."

"But it hasn't got to go on, has it?" Ann demanded tensely. "Rod, tell me the truth!"

"It will go on. Time is going backwards, and unless a miracle happens, it will continue to do so—" he ceased speaking as Ann suddenly threw her arms round him. He held her close for a very long time.

* * * * * * *

The biggest catastrophes in history, the greatest storms, the most extensive floods, and the worst earthquakes...all paled into entire insignificance by comparison with this new and titanic problem, which smote the world when Mankind tried to resume normalcy.

Although, ordinarily, it would have been New Year's day, the disturbances manifest at home led most people to investigate further. On every hand they encountered the solid wall of stagnation. Everything had come to an end.

Baffled newspaper editors surveyed mute telephones, sat indeed before desks that had upon them constantly shifting papers, all passing through the motions the editor himself had created for them in preceding time. When telephones could not even be handled, newspaper presses started on their own account and printed the previous day's news—which came out in reverse, gradually vanishing line by line—and even one's prized cigars could not be touched, the entire literary section of the world panicked. Reporters stranded in forsaken spots near various nerve-centers of the Earth wandered around in a daze, desperately trying to fathom how he or she could bring the news to the ears of their respective editors. They were quite unaware that the same events were in force the world over.

The ships at sea had the most uncanny experience of all.

When Time had ended they had suddenly stopped in their forward movement, and instead traveled as though through a hazy cloud. Within the cloud, there was very little sense of motion. Finally they entered mundane surroundings again at the point where they had started. Hardly had the passengers had time to jump ashore—by any means they could, for gang-planks could not be used—before the various ships involved had mysteriously faded and vanished, pursuing an ever backward course along the journeys they had previously made. In some instances hundreds of people were taken with them, literally swept into the limbo of forgotten things.

Tragedy, multiple and ever-mounting, stalked across the reversed world.

Similarly curious happenings occurred with trains. They merged back to their starting point. Porters and platelayers alike found it impossible to proceed with their usual work. Nobody seemed to know whether it was yesterday, today or tomorrow.

Other happenings were embarrassing rather than tragic. The world over, people found themselves changing clothes without visible aid. They found themselves in night and day clothes at unexpected moments, as they passed again—so far as the clothes were concerned—over the identical seconds. One leading politician left his home immaculate when Time changed to attend a New Year party of Top People. The later reversal in time finally brought him to wearing running shorts, in which he had performed slimming exercises before leaving his residence. Fortunately it was quite impossible to print his remarks.

Once the shiftings and returnings had to some extent passed away, the fact became evident that nothing could move forward. All cars went, driverless, through hazy backward movements to their garages or starting points. Then they reappeared in streets, only to fade again, ceaselessly. In several cases, new autos and locomotives reappeared in the makers' shops and engine-sheds respectively, after which they went through a steady process of dismantlement of their own accord. Their various parts were apparently lost as they moved back to their original state....

The only people on Earth who were not mightily handicapped were the astronomers. Their telescopes, guided to follow the heavens by clockwork, naturally went backwards in keeping with the similar backward motion of the solar system. Unfortunately three famous astronomers became mildly insane trying to solve the riddle; others went on desperately trying to compute what had occurred. So far as they could make out, time was moving faster, backwards, the earth apparently revolving now at just over twenty hours, against the old twenty-four. Man, trained from infancy to realize how long a day was, failed utterly to understand why the sun had taken to rising in the west, or why it moved so rapidly across the winter heavens.

The astronomers tried to communicate their knowledge to the press, with no success. They had to resort to word of mouth. Radio, of course, was equally useless. The ancient process of sending news by runners was revived. Trained athletes volunteered to do the work for a given fee, ran countless miles across the vibratory floor with which the world was covered. Ran, only to discover that not only could their fee not be given them, but it would have been useless even if it could....

Gradually, Man began to realize the cardinal tragedy that had struck him.

Although, in a literal sense, it was a world without progress, events were happening constantly. Everywhere, every minute, the skyline was changing. Buildings that had been pulled down were reappearing by degrees; others were disappearing. No longer was it safe to go anywhere, so various populations prepared for migration to the open spaces where they would at least stand a chance.

Finding that animals could be obtained and killed, Man did not need further instruction. Sheep were strangled by strong men, and despite an initial repugnance, had to be eaten raw. Fire would not kindle, so cooking was out. These methods applied chiefly to the vast average classes, who were stricken with mortal panic. The more intelligent remained behind in the changing, baffling cities to try and think out other methods of

procedure.

Since no known cosmic law fitted in with the reversal in Time, scientists began to claim that the occurrence was not a natural one. So, once again, messengers were sent amongst the people, demanding that the creator of this disaster should come forward. The news failed to reach Doctor Thurman himself, but it did reach Bertie Vincent. Vincent, having already been scared out of his few wits by these proceedings, sought the local police chief of the New York East Division.

"I tell you he's a madman!" he declared to Chief Inspector Barker, when he had finally managed to enter the police station. "With my own eyes I saw the machine switched on. After that clocks started to go backwards."

"You wouldn't try to fool me, would you?" the chief asked heavily. "God knows I've had enough explanations about this nutty business. Still, you might just have something. Where can I find this Doctor Thurman?"

"I'll take you to him."

For a moment the chief considered, then nodded. "Okay, I'll come with you. Guess we'll have to walk; the auto's no use. Come on."

Fifteen minutes brought them to the Doctor's home and Barker hammered imperiously on the door. At least, this was what he tried to do, but the invisible vibration between only stung his knuckles and gave forth no sound.

"Hell!" he muttered, nursing his tingling knuckles. "Guess this infernal invisible stuff is enough to drive a guy out of his mind. What are we—?"

He broke off, staring, as he caught a glimpse of a round face and bald head through the glass of the bay window. It disappeared almost instantly, then a voice came from beyond the front door.

"I can let you in as soon as the door opens," Thurman shouted. "Sorry, but that's all there is for it."

"Darned humbug," the officer growled, then cocked a suspicious eye on Bertie. "Say, how did you get into the police station

when doors can't be opened by ordinary methods?"

"Probably because the door of the police station is rarely shut—not in the big centers, anyhow," Bertie replied mildly. Barker gave a grunt of disgust.

"Okay, so we wait," he said. Then, after a pause, in an odd voice, he added: "Do you have much difficulty with your clothes?"

"Sure I do. They keep changing without me doing anything— but I'm getting used to it. By roughly calculating the time backwards I can tell when the change will come and what I'll have on. The biggest worry though is food. I haven't had a bite to eat, or a drink since—Oh, I don't know when. A long time."

"Same here," the officer growled. "My wife and kids, and myself; we haven't had a thing since New Year's Eve. Guess this crazy guy in here's got a lot to answer for— Hey, quick! The door's opening!"

He stood alert as he saw the knob turn, then as the door swung back he charged into the hall with Bertie beside him. A moment later the door swung closed again.

Bertie saw that the Doctor himself, Ann and Rodney were all present in the hall. attired exactly as they had been at that time two days ago. Hence Thurman was in an overall stained with chemicals, Ann in a greasy old dress in which she had been cleaning her small runabout, and Rodney in a comparatively respectable everyday suit. Then, even as the astounded officer and Bertie watched, Rodney's tie suddenly changed from a bright new one to an old and faded one. The young man grinned slightly as he noticed the change. Of course, he *had* changed the wretched thing. The new one he had bought was now gone forever.

"Which of you two gentlemen is Doctor Thurman?" the officer demanded, nearly closing one eye—evidently under the impression this facial distortion would add weight to his enquiry.

Thurman stepped forward. "I am, inspector. Why?"

"This gentleman here tells me you're responsible for the

unholy mess that's going on. Is that right?"

"Bertie, you damned—" began Rodney, clenching his fist.

"Well, I didn't see any harm in telling him!" Bertie protested. "After all, the creator of the trouble was asked to step forward. I got wind of it and told the police."

"Why couldn't you have told me?" Thurman demanded.

"Well—er—"

"I know, you thought I was safer under lock and key, eh?" Thurman smiled bitterly. "I know you think I'm half mad, Bertie; you always did. Well, what if I am? What do you propose doing, officer? Certainly I made the machine that is the cause of this trouble, but it was an accident that started the whole thing."

"Scientists are asking you to step forward and try to see what can be done to remedy things," the inspector explained carefully. "Are you prepared to do so?"

"I would do so willingly if there was a ghost of a chance of righting things—but there isn't. I know—to my cost!"

"Then I'll have to put you in charge," the inspector declared flatly. "I still have my duty to do."

"You mean put me in prison?" Thurman asked quietly, then he burst into a chuckle as Chief Inspector Barker nodded complacently.

"What's so funny?"

"Just that you can't do a thing! Don't you realize that we're plunging backwards in time? You can't get hold of anything; you can't do anything. Why, before very long, the very prisons themselves will be falling to pieces; arriving back at the time they were built."

"Hell, I never thought of that." Barker was dazed. "It's the same sort of thing that stops us eating, isn't it?"

Thurman seemed to decide something. "Haven't you had any food since this thing began?" he asked quietly.

"No, neither me nor my family. I don't know how much longer we can go on."

"I've had nothing, either," remarked Bertie aggrievedly.

"If I give you a cold chicken, inspector, and a gourd of milk—

unfortunately sour, but none the less drinkable—will you do me a favor?"

"Depends what it is."

"You can't pick and choose, my friend. An empty stomach and a starving family are ruthless masters. Law and order have gone by the board, and we are all creatures facing a common foe—existence! I'm willing to give you food and drink to take home with you, in return for a service."

For an instant Barker hesitated; then he nodded, "Okay—what is it?"

"At the moment you still have some vestiges of authority. I want you to round up as many of your men as you can. Next, get all the civilians you can contact between you into the park opposite my home here. Can you do that, Inspector?"

"I guess so. But what—"

"I want to address them," Thurman interrupted impatiently. "It's time the people of this city at least knew what they were facing. Get all the people you can into the park by sunset. Sunset in the east, of course."

"All right, Doctor. I'll do my best. Meantime...."

Thurman smiled. "Ah, yes, the food. Come this way you too, Bertie. I'll see that you get something as well. Even though you are nothing but a damned nuisance. Still, you've done an unwitting good turn."

Rodney and Ann, left alone in the hall, glanced at each other.

"Rod, where is all this going to end? The strain of trying to remember what happened on such-and-such a day is appalling. I just can't keep it up!"

"You were cleaning your car," Rodney smiled. "Your clothes prove it. It's no use worrying about it, Ann. Pretty soon nobody will be able to remember a thing with any certainty. Only thing is to try and remember the most important happenings, and prepare for them coming back."

"To think I helped to cause it," Ann murmured in a low voice. For a moment she was close to tears. "Oh Rod, I wish I was going backwards in Time as well—then I'd return to zero

and be no more. What is there left to live for in a world like this? For me—the one who brought it all about?"

Rodney looked at her fixedly. "Don't talk like that," he said quietly. "Besides, who knows, in the end we might start going forward again. There's also the chance of humans becoming affected eventually. Your father mentioned the possibility, you know."

"It's all horrible!" Ann was near to tears again, then she paused as her father returned.

"Well, they've both gone," Thurman announced. "Had to wait for the rear door to open. I gave them a gourd of our milk and some cold chicken between them—I think Bertie's got some idea of living in with him. Like everybody else, it doesn't matter where he lives. There's no family life any more."

"This meeting," Rodney asked, "what's the idea of it?"

"If I can get some of the people together, then I stand a chance to try and formulate some new laws to meet the emergency. As instigator of this mess, it's up to me to do something. Mankind will have to return to tribal law.

"Ultimately, if things go on, there'll be no cities—nothing. Even the land will start to change, because the backward rate is increasing enormously. The days and nights are becoming shorter. The whole thing is ghastly—I don't like it!"

"Who does?" Ann asked bitterly.

* * * * * * *

Chief Inspector Barker, after a brief triumphal return home with the foodstuffs, kept his promise. He and such other policemen who had reported for duty duly proceeded to herd all the civilians within sight into Willow Park. Sick with hunger and bafflement, they offered little protest. The sight of his uniform and the promise that a scientist would speak to them, try and aid them, was sufficient to instill obedience. By sundown the park was packed, and Thurman himself, Ann and Rodney beside him, eventually arrived.

Thurman selected a disused fountain for an address platform, and by dint of hoarse shouting, tried to make clear to the multitude what had happened.

"We are at a point in human life where science cannot aid us!" he shouted, husky with voice-strain. "We have only two means of sustenance—milk and animals. With our bare hands we shall have to kill sheep, hens, rabbits, pigs, and so forth. I doubt if any of us can kill a cow or horse bare-handed, but we might as well try it. We cannot use instruments to aid us.

"You are finding your clothes constantly changing. When your stock of clothes has run out, which they will do rapidly because we are living slower than the Change about us, you will find yourselves stark naked. Those of you who can obtain fur coats had better do so; steal them if need be. They alone will not disappear, because they belong to an organic animal."

"Why fur coats, with summer coming?" yelled a voice.

Thurman gestured impatiently. "When will you people realize that everything is in reverse?" he demanded. "The reversal started on December 31st; it is not now January 4th, but December 28th! We've got to live back through the winter we've passed. Seasons are now exactly the opposite."

"Where we going to live? What are we going to do?" screamed a woman near the front of the crowd.

"You can all go to your respective homes," Thurman answered. "They will be safe enough until such time as they were first built; after that they will vanish, of course.... The strongest amongst you must get to work right away and obtain food. What you obtain can be placed in the nearest abattoirs—then inform me. We can then try and work out some method of distribution."

"And milk?" yelled a voice.

"Obtain it from any cows or goats in all the natural leather objects you can find—handbags, gloves, pure hide attaché cases—anything made of animal skin. The animals' milk must be run directly into the containers."

"So we've got to eat raw meat, huh?" demanded a truculent

voice, revealed as a hulking ruffian in the middle distance. "Say, professor, what do you take us for? Damned animals?"

Thurman compressed his lips bitterly.

"You can't make fire to cook it," he snapped. "Why do you ask such idiotic questions? You know by now that nothing that progresses can be touched or worked."

"Fire *can* be produced, Doctor," called a powerfully-built man on his left; then as Thurman stared at him in surprise as he came forward and vaulted lightly to the fountain. He turned to address the people.

"I grant that fire is impossible by ordinary methods," boomed his strong voice. "You have all probably used, or tried to, firewood—matches—and coal. Naturally nothing could be touched. All the same I've made a fire in my home." He paused dramatically, breathing hard, conscious of the people hanging on his every word.

"I ran out of food recently, so I killed off one of my pigs using my bare hands. Half of the pig's fatty flesh I used for fuel, and some of the bones as well. A couple of the bones rubbed rapidly together produced enough friction in time to create fire and set the fat alight. Since it was flesh and blood it lit perfectly. Then I was able to cook the remaining half of the pig." Thurman, who had been looking thoughtful, touched him on the arm, and made to speak himself.

"I've just thought of another method, going from what our friend here has been saying. However, it requires sunlight and won't be nearly so effective. The eye of a pig could act as a magnifying glass, and it's possible to focus the sun's rays on the pig, in sections. But the bone-rubbing idea is a good one, and should be tried."

"I never thought of that," the man remarked. Then, realizing his moment had passed, and that he had nothing more useful to add, he jumped down into the crowd again and awaited Thurman's further instructions.

"So make fires!" Thurman shouted. "For the moment there is nothing more that can be decided upon. I'll leave you to obtain

the food as I've suggested, and then I'll help you arrange distribution later."

Whether the people were satisfied or not could not altogether be determined. But Thurman reasoned that he had done all in his power to clear up the main problem—food and drink. The rest would have to come later. To reorganize Man's entire mode of living would take considerable time....

"Guess you did your best, Doc," Rodney murmured, watching the people slowly dispersing. "Some of them will probably resent your self-appointed position as leader—but someone had to make the move."

"You did remarkably well," commented a strong voice. Turning in surprise, the trio beheld the inventor of the fire-making system beside them. His sharply chiseled intelligent face had a dry smile upon it. "Joseph Mason is my name," he volunteered. "You may have heard of me."

"Joseph Mason," Thurman thought hard for a moment, then in some astonishment, "Why, you're a scientific writer of sorts, aren't you?"

"Um—yes, of sorts. Ordinarily I breed animals, but geology has always been a hobby with me. I once wrote a book: *Earth Through the Ages.*"

"Yes—yes, I recall it now. You revealed a remarkable knowledge of the past."

"Mainly a hobby with me. Unfortunately for me, my home was newly constructed, and now of course it is beginning to come to pieces. Perhaps I might join up with you? I'd rather be with people of a sane, scientific outlook than amongst the masses."

"You can join us with pleasure," Thurman said sincerely. "You're the sort of person I could do with—someone with ideas. Oh, excuse me—meet my daughter, Ann, and her husband Mr. Rodney Shenstone."

Mason shook hands, then remarked: "You know, Doctor, you certainly didn't think out this business at all well. You've burned your bridges behind you more effectually than any other

man in history. When one thinks of what you've done—"

"What I've done, you mean," Ann put in, her face coloring. "This is all my fault, Mr. Mason."

"A delusion she has, Mason," Thurman intervened hastily. "Come along to my home and we'll talk properly." He led the way through the park entrance and across the road. They waited as a driverless car swept uncannily past, then continued their journey. Followed a wait of some thirty minutes before the front door opened, then the Doctor led the way into the lounge. The rays of the eastwardly setting sun were still slanting into the room.

"These doors are a damned nuisance, aren't they?" Mason asked casually, looking about him. "I tried the expedient of putting my foot against the front door when it opened last time—but no! It shut just the same. My foot appeared to go through it, and yet oddly enough I was up against a solidity. Most paradoxical!"

"The whole business is mad—insane," Rodney declared. "I've been nursing a faint hope you might have some solution to the difficulty. Have you?"

Mason shook his head. "I'm sorry—no. It is beyond the power of man to right this phenomenon, even though the ingenuity of Man—you, Doctor—has reversed Time. If only you could have foreseen what might happen."

Thurman passed a weary hand over his forehead. "There's something about all this that is utterly maddening—overpowering. I wonder I keep my sanity."

"I did it!" Ann flared out suddenly. "I was drunk, Mr. Mason—drunk with New Year wine. I interfered with Dad's apparatus—and then the thing was done in a flash. I can never forgive myself for that. My hand wrecked progress! I—one woman—flung thousands, millions to their deaths by my muddle-headed, crazy actions. Oh, I wish to God that I were dead!"

"Steady, Ann," Rodney muttered, seizing her shoulder as she subsided into sobs.

"Yes, take it easy," Mason advised, and his very calmness of tone had a steadying effect on the overwrought girl. "No matter who did it, or how, it's happened: now we've got to face the results. It's surprising how Man can learn to fend for himself even when faced with this kind of thing."

"The fire stunt, for instance?" Rodney asked.

"Exactly so—but there are also nights when one hasn't happened to be at home, and hence the lighting is off. I've been trying to think of a way to overcome it. Only thing I can think of would be to try and obtain a considerable number of fish scales and use their luminescence."

Thurman shook his head at Mason's suggestion. "I think darkness would be preferable to that," he said dryly. "If there's one thing I detest, it's the smell of fish! Besides, it won't do. We can't catch any fish—which is why I did not suggest them as a source of food earlier. Between us and the sea is that invisible wall of vibration. The fish are there, all right, but we can't get at them. Like flies in amber." He fell silent, not wishing to dwell on the obvious.

"I've been thinking," Rodney put in. "Weren't you absent from your home for a day or so recently, Doctor?"

Thurman gave a slight start. "Yes, I'd almost forgotten. I see what you mean," he went on grimly. "During that period the lights would be switched off, so we'll just have to sit in the dark."

"So what?" Ann asked, then added bitterly: "At least I won't be able to look at myself."

"Why don't you and Ann fetch some of our food and milk supplies, Rod?" Thurman said, sensing that Ann was on the point of another outburst. "Bring it over to the settee; it hasn't been moved in a while so we'll be safe enough on it. I hope you won't mind sour milk, Mason?"

"I thrive on it, Doctor."

It was almost dark when Rodney and Ann reappeared, dimly visible carrying the remains of a turkey in their hands. Plates of course, were impossible, as the crockery couldn't be in two

places at once. With every reverting second, Man was becoming surrounded by complicated, incredible circumstances.

Silently. Ann sat down, holding her own piece of turkey absently. Only when Rodney's arm stole round her waist did she start back into life; then she munched steadily, but listlessly.

In the interval that followed, there were several halfhearted attempts to steer the conversation onto ordinary topics, but no one responded. The factor of Time reversal was the one over-powering thought on their minds. Finally Mason voiced his real thoughts.

"It's clear to me from my watch, and the shortening day and night periods, that this reversal is increasing with every passing hour. Finally we'll get four ordinary days in the space of twenty-four hours. Then faster still, until the sun will look something like a band of golden light. We shall live in a world of perpetual change. Lost in chaos...." He snapped the turkey bone between strong teeth.

"But, Mr. Mason, there is surely *some* answer?" Ann entreated. "Although dad's so clever at thinking out these scien-tific miracles, he's just hopeless when it comes to undoing the messes he creates. Perhaps someone with more sense than he has—"

"Ann!"

"I mean it, father—and you know I'm right. Mr Mason, are you sure that scientists somewhere won't be able to put things right?"

"Young lady, there is no way," Mason replied steadily. "It's like a poison without an antidote. Your father's experiment was so clever he defeated his own ends and everybody else."

"So science admits defeat that easily!" Ann said disgustedly.

There was an uncomfortable silence, then presently Mason resumed.

"At the rate we shall shortly find Time moving, we might be able to view the world as it was before the coming of Man. In a way that will be interesting. Ultimately, thousands of years will hurtle past us in the space of a few hours. So, Earth's early days

will catch up with us."

"Then—then we shall finally come to the place where Earth is no longer in existence!" Rod remarked suddenly, a note of horror in his voice.

"Certainly," Mason assented philosophically. "We shall, I hope, see everything. The moon's return to Earth—if indeed it was ever part of this planet; the upheavals of the early days. Last of all will come Earth's return to the cosmic gases from which it sprang, though I doubt if we'll be here to view that!"

"I wonder if humanity at large realizes what is to come?" Thurman muttered, and Mason laughed.

"Of course not!" he said cynically. "Most people think the whole thing is going to blow over, whereas the very worst is not even in sight yet. Think what it means—the procession of Ages in reverse! Everything from the Quaternary Epoch to the Silurian Period! And then beyond that into the unknown! I doubt if we'll survive."

"I, for one, don't want to," Ann said quietly.

"You say that now, but the very fascination of these changes will make death seem distasteful," Mason said. "Those that can survive will behold the most astounding things. Since we four have a fair knowledge of things between us, we may survive longer than the majority. Eh, Doctor?"

"It hardly bears thinking about," Thurman grunted. "I've had quite enough worry for one day. To be brief, I'm going to try and sleep. Are you two coming?" He rose to his feet and glanced at Rodney and Ann in the gloom.

"Later," Rodney replied quietly. "I want to talk to Ann for a while."

"Just as you like. Come along, Mason—I'll show you to your room. But 1 accept no responsibility for what might happen in it! Goodnight you two."

Low voices answered him. When they were alone, Rodney took his wife's hand, looking at her face in the faint starlight.

"Ann, I want you to promise me that you'll do nothing rash," he said firmly. "I mean that—Well, the way you've been talking,

you seem convinced that you're the cause of all this. Thinking that, you might do something tragic."

"Meaning?" Ann asked listlessly.

"You wouldn't be foolish enough to—to kill yourself, would you?" Rodney forced the words out with distaste. "It has happened, you know, when people have got unstrung."

"Kill myself?" The girl jolted upright, withdrew her hand from Rodney's grasp-then abruptly burst into peal upon peal of hysterical laughter.

"Ann! Stop it! *Stop it*!" Rodney clutched her shoulders and shook her violently. Presently Ann seemed to calm down a little. Her voice broke somewhat between weariness and emotional laughter as she spoke again.

"I can't kill myself! If I could, I would, Rodney. Yes, I *would!* The memory of my crime will remain forever. But Heaven knows I'm being punished enough for it!"

"Ann—" Rodney was utterly at a loss.

"I can't seize a knife, I can't obtain a revolver, I can't drink poison. I can't even drown myself, because I can't displace the water or something stupid like that! It's the same for all of us; those who suffer. I long for self-inflicted death to escape this world, but nothing can happen. I'm a woman who cannot die, unless...unless!" Hysteria gripped her again as Rodney held her shoulders. *"You!"* she breathed hoarsely. "You can do it for me, Rodney. You could strangle me, or—*oh*!" her words were snapped off as his hand slapped across her face.

"You're going to see it through! Don't talk like that!" Rodney shouted, sweat beading his brow. Ann collapsed against him, sobbing helplessly.

"Take it easy," he whispered, his sense of outrage evaporating as he realized, fully and completely, the ordeal his wife was facing.

He took her in his arms, raising her bodily, and walked steadily towards the now open door of the room.

* * * * * * *

During the incredible days that followed, Man became increasingly aware of the true enormity of the thing that had come upon him. In many areas he reverted to bestial savagery, even cannibalism. But in New York, at least, some people followed out Doctor Thurman's suggestions, as a small body of men set to work killing off various animals by main strength. Fires, too, were provided by means of the method Mason had discovered.

Aided by Mason, Thurman himself supervised the food distribution in the main city abattoirs.

It was a gigantic task. Milk, too, was duly obtained in many weird and varied vessels. So, for a time at least, the seething queues of people were supplied with food and drink.

A strange and motley array of people they proved to be. Arriving ceaselessly, and occasionally exploding into violence—immediately choked off by gangs of dedicated attendants—some dressed in clothes that were remarkably new; yet the men were unshaven and the women grimy. A few of the more fastidious people used some of the milk for washing purposes, others grease. The vast majority went filthy and unwashed.

For six days this system of feeding and drinking persisted—then the blow fell, relentlessly and completely. Not surprisingly it was the imperturbable Mason who made the discovery.

"Doc, the game's up," he announced to his three soiled and troubled colleagues, in Thurman's home. "I've been out making a few investigations on my own account, and I've discovered something we'd overlooked. Cattle are dying everywhere, rapidly, because there is no natural food or water. None of the animals can eat grass or drink water!"

"Can't we feed them on the meat of other cattle?" Rodney demanded.

"Useless to try. For one thing no cow will eat cow, nor horse eat horse. For another it's the wrong food entirely."

"So the source of nourishment has dried up," Thurman said somberly. "Well, we've got to look out for ourselves now; leave the people to do what they can. Nothing else for it."

"We've got to get out before the people realize what's wrong," Mason had evidently been thinking ahead. "They'll lynch us when they find out what's happened." He broke off, regarding Thurman and Rodney each in turn.

"You two look different somehow," he remarked, frowning. Then he shrugged. "Come on—we'll collect what food we've got, our milk gourds, and then get out."

"Where to?" Ann asked.

"Anywhere! We'll worry about that when we're safe from the people in the vicinity. Come on."

He strode in the direction of the larder, which was open, and seized two heavy milk gourds. He slung them over his shoulder by the tough cow-gut thong that joined them. Silently the others collected up what remains of food they could find, and turned to leave.

"These are going to be an infernal weight to lug around," Mason muttered, heaving at the milk-gourds. "I wonder if there's a better way...." he rubbed his jaw absently, then gave a yelp. To the astonishment of the others he began to pat his face rapidly, a wild light in his eyes.

"What's the matter?" Thurman demanded.

Mason dropped the milk-gourds heavily to the vibration-level that passed for the floor. He looked considerably shaken.

"Now I know why you two looked different! Your beards have gone!"

Blankly, the two men fingered their jaws.

"I noticed mine had gone when I stroked my chin just now," Mason went on. "I've been trying to place the difference in you two for some time. Funny how long it took to spot it. We're all of us without beards!"

"But how could that be, if you haven't shaved?" Ann asked in bewilderment.

"It's obvious now," Thurman said grimly. "I knew all along that my machine's vibrations would finally affect living organisms as well. This is the beginning! We're going backwards, too—much slower than the giant reversal around us, because

we're organic. Our beards have grown backwards, as it were, and all we'll get in future will be the small sproutings corresponding to those prior to shaving—and they'll vanish pretty rapidly. One thing is obvious, though. We need no food and no water. A state of backward growth requires no nourishment; metabolism has ceased. No tissue wastage! We probably won't sleep either, since sleep is caused chiefly by tissue-waste products in the blood—and now there is none."

"Now that we're growing younger, will we repeat all our bodily troubles?" Rodney asked. "I once broke an ankle, years ago, at a sports meeting."

"I don't think so. The external Time conditions don't correspond with the conditions we experienced in past life. We shouldn't repeat illnesses, injuries, or such like because external Time is moving so fast compared to us. We can never catch up with the conditions that caused those things. We'll simply grow younger constantly...."

Mason was seemingly elated at the weird prospect facing them. "Which means we're free to do anything we want, go where we want, see what we want—so long as our bodies remain."

"Of course," Thurman agreed. "We can't even be injured, so far as I can see—otherwise those injuries would already be recorded. You could say we're eternal—backwards!'

"A living tomb," Ann muttered. "We cannot die meanwhile, yet in the end we must do, because we'll be too young to live!"

"A merciful finish," said Mason, now looking thoughtful.

"Well, let's get out. Nothing stopping us is there?" Rodney asked.

Followed the customary waiting period, then when the door ultimately did open, the four crossed the threshold into the street. It took a good deal of will on the part of Thurman in particular to leave the place for the last time. He had spent all of his married life in the house, including also the last seven years following the death of his wife.

"Which way?" Rodney asked, glancing about him.

"It doesn't really signify, so long as we move away from the docks area—Hallo! This looks ugly!" Mason broke off.

Round the corner of the avenue there had suddenly appeared a motley collection of determined civilians. They had borne down on Thurman and his party before they could make the effort to run for it. Grimy hands reached out and seized them.

"You, Thurman, are the one we want!" snarled the self-appointed leader of the mob. "You knew our food and drink would fail! Now you're trying to escape, leaving us to starve: get that stuff off them!" he snapped, and the four found their food and drink supply snatched from them.

"Listen to reason, man!" Thurman panted, trying to pull himself loose. "If you'll only try to—"

"Aw, can the excuses! How are we going to live? That's all that interests us!"

The crowd grew visibly with the seconds, and Thurman looked about him uneasily. There was no telling how a vicious public, facing starvation and believing they had been duped, might react.

"Leave go of my wife, can't you?" Rodney shouted, as several hulking specimens pulled at her struggling form. Fears of muti-lation and rape snapped through his racing brain. Abruptly he stamped down onto the foot of the ruffian who was pinioning his arms. His foot seemed to pass clean through the man. Startled, he relaxed his grip. Instantly Rodney lashed out at the roughneck clutching his wife. The man was sent reeling but did not appear hurt. A moment later Rodney went down under the weight of several bodies.

"That settles it!" their leader snapped. "We get rid of 'em—now!"

"Throw 'em in the sea!" somebody yelled.

"The sea! The sea!" reiterated countless hoarse voices.

"Can't you fools realize anything?" Mason panted, strug-gling desperately. "Don't you know you're getting younger—?"

"Hear that?" bawled a derisive voice. "We're getting younger! If that isn't a laugh I don't know what is!"

"We're sick of explanations, buddy, and we mean to have action," said the leader grimly. "Guess we'll get on better without you four creeps for a start. Okay, boys, lift 'em up!"

The four were instantly seized with eager hands, lifted aloft, and carried in triumph through the mob-lined streets. They were swept along towards the main docks about the city's harbor. Presently the quartet was flung down at the edge of a high landing stage. From below came the curiously revolting sound of waves lapping in reverse.

"You've asked for this!" growled the leader thickly. "You've been the cause of all our troubles, and now you're going to pay." He swung round on his comrades. "In with 'em!" he bawled harshly. "It'll be dark in a moment or two. Hurry it up!"

"What if they swim ashore?" said one of the burly figures.

"Aw, use your brains. The tides are always haywire these days and will sweep 'em out. Besides, we'll soon finish them if they try and get out. These walls are sheer anyhow. Okay, throw 'em in!"

"Wait—" began Thurman desperately, but that was as far as he got. The next moment he was knocked into space by a violent push. Likewise Ann, Rodney and Mason. They were completely helpless against the mob, and plummeted down into the gloomy abyss of the dock.

Those above them stood listening intently, but no sound of a splash reached them. Anxiously they peered into the murk— then came a discontented voice.

"What's the use of standing here in the dark? They've gone all right. Let's get back to the city and try and find some more food and drink. The stuff those rats had won't do for more than a few of us."

"Yeah. Maybe you're right," the leader was strangely hesitant. "Funny thing; I don't feel either hungry or thirsty.... We'll get back, all the same."

And he strode forward purposefully, leading his filthy band back towards the unfamiliar, slowly vanishing skyline of New York.

* * * * * * *

Four figures rose up very slowly and perplexedly in the
darkness at the bottom of the dock wall. Beneath their feet
was complete solidity. Yet, faintly visible, apparently passing
through their legs and clothes without leaving any impression,
were the waves of the sea. For several moments they had been
too frightened to move, which fact had probably saved them
from further mob action. Thurman gave a quiet chuckle.

"Of course!" he exclaimed. "We can't enter water because
we'd be displacing it in a time where it hasn't formerly been
displaced. It's the same effect here as on land; everything is
separated by vibration. Literally, we are walking on water....
Hmm, wonder if that had anything to do with Biblical miracles?"

"But we're not even hurt after our fall down here!" Ann was
dazed by events, if not by her fall.

"Of course not," Mason answered her. "Since we are growing
younger with every second we can't be damaged by anything—
otherwise we'd contravene Time. We remain sound in body
because that's how we were back at this moment in Time."

"This possibility of walking unharmed on the sea, and being
unable to be injured in any way, opens up boundless possibilities," Thurman remarked, after an interval. "If we go back to
the city, we'd be set upon again by the mob. And even though
we couldn't be killed, the experience is unlikely to be pleasant.
Personally, therefore, I propose going to Europe."

"Europe!" Rodney echoed blankly. "You mean walk two
thousand miles across the ocean?"

"Why not? We've got the rest of our backward lives to do
it in, and nothing can stop us. Besides, some of the greatest
geological events took place in Europe. Lots of things there
might be worth seeing, eh Mason?"

"It's a great idea, Doc!" Mason agreed. "We'll do it. Apart
from anything else, we're not likely to be troubled much by any
wandering mobs out here on the ocean. Okay with you two?"

Rodney shrugged and took Ann's arm. "Lead the way."

"Moon's rising," remarked Ann, pointing to the west. "It'll light the way."

So began perhaps the most amazing journey ever made by mortal creatures. Walking on the surface of the waves, untroubled by the ebbing rollers that passed through them as they went. Four mortals whose clothes still changed periodically no matter how far they traveled from their home; clothes that became slowly newer. And even the mind of Thurman was yet to grasp the full enormity of the incredible events.

* * * * * * *

As the days slid by into weeks, and weeks into months, the full effects of the Time reversal became manifest. Within two months—by the old reckoning—of the coming of the reversal there was no recognized night and day. Only an utterly confusing rapidly accelerating backward sweep through the ages.

The sun appeared now as a golden ball, hurtling west-to-east, to be followed by the violently phasing moon in reverse. The whole heavens were darkly purple—a mass of crisscrossing hazes of light. And even some of the nearer stars seemed to eddy and shift position.

New York itself had dwindled to zero, as had a great many other cities and towns. Everything began to recede from the face of the Earth as Man's handiwork disappeared into the sealed vault that was future time. Man watched and wondered, dazed and bewildered. He had found by now that he was growing younger, no longer needed nourishment or sleep. This knowledge scarcely eased the minds of the masses. However, no one suffered from insanity or mental breakdowns, simply because they never had done so.

Vegetation, growing in reverse, began to appear as an untouchable mass of spewing, spreading and receding green, Gradually it overtook and covered the over the vast, open rocky spaces where once proud cities had reared up. Mountains

rose—and fell. At times humans would find themselves plunged to enormous depths or raised to stupendous heights by shiftings of the ground on which they stood—only somehow they avoided injury.

So the change went on, the world over, at an ever increasing speed. And out on the swirling bosom of the Atlantic, four human beings continued their march towards Europe. All of them were now some three years younger than when they had started. They were naked. Owing to the lapse of external Time, their clothes had long since failed them. Rodney, in a brief and abortive attempt to save his wife's modesty, had made attempts to utilize the skins of the countless fish they encountered. But the fish were just *in* the water to keep them alive, just as human beings could still breathe the atmosphere around them, and were separated from actual contact by the vibration above the water. But before long, so utterly had normal standards of civilization and modesty been shattered, they adapted to their condition. Indeed they wondered as they progressed why Man had ever bothered with clothes at all.

As the trek continued, it became evident that the Atlantic was rapidly receding, as they encountered a profusion of bone-dry islands. Ultimately, upon a vast and lonely island in the midst of the all-pervading yellowish glow of the streaking sun, they beheld an incredible sight.

Surrounded by the thundering breakers of the untouchable ocean stood a city of dreams, dry and majestic. Mighty pyramids and slender towers stood side by side in a system of architecture and structural brilliance such as had never been seen by any of the quartet. It looked at once incredibly ancient but somehow ultra-modern, like a city of the future might have looked.

"What is it?" breathed Mason. "Anything you know, Thurman?"

"It must be Atlantis!" Thurman cried. "It was supposed to exist somewhere off Northern Europe, wasn't it? Just look at those pillars—those edifices! And yet no people...."

"Nothing that has died becomes visible."

For perhaps half an hour of ordinary time, the four stood staring at the apparition from Time—a half hour in which centuries streaked backwards. Then, piece by piece, the city visibly crumbled, diminished—a reverse action of it being built by hands no longer apparent. At last it became entirely ghostlike, merged into the mists of the unknown, and was gone. The island upon which it had stood grew visibly then, rose up steadily, and spread out dry feelers through the receding ocean. Presently the four watchers realized they were on dry ground.

"Which shows geological theories to be correct," commented Mason. "Northern Europe *did* extend far out into the modern Atlantic Ocean. North-Western Europe, to be exact.... Well, Thurman, now that we're here, are you satisfied?"

"More than satisfied," the scientist answered quietly. "We may behold many things now that we are here. Let's be moving on."

So the advance continued. Ever and again they came across drifting tribes of naked men and women, wandering along the hardened and solidified plains of this remotely early land. Here they detoured, having elected to keep rigidly to themselves. In many ways it was an unpleasant land, frozen in many parts later on, concurring, according to Mason, with the arrival of the Glacial Period. Soon they would actually arrive at the period of the Earth before Man himself had come to be.

"How can that be?" Rodney asked, when Mason made the point. "We can't reach that early on, otherwise we'd be confounding our own birthright."

"I thought you understood by now that we move thousands of times slower than external Time," Mason responded. "We're growing younger, but at this rate Earth will be nearly back to cosmic dust before we ourselves become extinct."

"Where do we go now?" Ann asked. As Mason had predicted, she was alertly interested in the things around her. Her crushing self-guilt was hardly evident. "Funny how we're nearly standing on ice and yet feel no cold, isn't it?"

"That's because everything about us, although real enough

in itself, is just like a vivid dream would be to us," Thurman returned slowly. His gaze swept the friendless gray level plain before him. "We'll go across the plain ahead of us, and see where it brings us."

For many normal weeks they wandered haphazardly, going wherever the mood took them. Everywhere about them was perpetual backward change. Finally they arrived in a region that had once been a mountain range in Norway. From a high elevation they beheld something that astounded them, impressing Mason particularly.

The valley below them, through which they had come, had been filled to the topmost foothills with ice-packed water. Yet now, as they watched, the whole vast sea of ice and mud was boiling strangely. The curious condition persisted and became even more agitated as the time reversal progressed. Then, in one thundering, boiling mass the whole sea began to drop, leaving dry land below it. The waters surged and battered their way through a stupendous chasm in the far end of the mountain range, carrying back boulders of ice and snow in their grip. Finally there was left a peaceful, deserted valley, dry as a board. No trace of a cleft remained in the mountain range that had resealed itself.

"What on earth happened?" demanded Rodney at last, and Mason smiled faintly in the yellow light.

"That was the North European deluge in reverse," he answered. "I wondered if something like this wouldn't happen as we crossed the vast mass of water that existed in the valley down there. It didn't strike me as a natural place for an inland sea at the time."

"Do you mean it was *the* Deluge, that was in the Bible?" Ann enquired excitedly.

Mason smiled. "No; just one of several deluges that swept the Earth in early times. The Biblical Deluge came long after Man had arrived; this age is before Man. We missed that, being in the wrong part of the world. What did you make of it, Thurman?"

"Very queer, especially as it has left bone dry land behind. Of course it was bound to do so, because now we see the land before the deluge came."

After an interval, they continued over the mountain range. On and on they traveled, for no other reason than to see where it might bring them.

* * * * * * *

As the backward flight became even more rapid, so the change in human organisms increased its pace. As a result all Mankind was becoming visibly younger.

By the time Thurman's party had crossed the range to the pre-deluge plain beyond, they were quite six years younger than at their departure from New York. Ann had receded into a slim, girlish creature; Rodney into a young man of immature appearance. Mason had lost considerable bulk. Thurman, too, had lost his stoop of incipient age. He walked now with a springy step and much more erect carriage.

Their wanderings brought them to the Europe of the Quaternary Epoch. They no longer beheld flat plains, but varied mountain ranges, and not a little vegetation. Forests came and went with succeeding ice ages. Such hardy trees as oaks and willows were in evidence, passing from full growth into saplings, then entirely disappearing. Then silent and untouchable, the Epoch slid into scenes of the Pliocene Period, and a more temperate zone. The land was remarkably green and restful for a space. Rivers flowed backwards in the shifting landscape. They passed safely through a tremendous upheaval that Mason imagined to be the formation of the North Sea itself.

Here and there were vast lakes and inland seas, many of which would remain in modified form in time to come—if indeed the future could still be regarded as such.

In the main, they had noticed, the skies had been clear. True, clouds had transiently arrived, but they were gone in a flash, even though they might have persisted in actuality for a decade. For the most part the deeply purple heavens remained unmarred; and, on the changing Earth below, the Miocene and Eocene Periods came and went, to give way to the crueler looking stretches of the Cretaceous Period. The landscape had changed enormously; the ever-ebbing sea had come inwards and washed now against swampy coastal plains, forming enormous deltas.

By the time Ann had regressed to fifteen and Rodney eighteen they had all four come to the swampy, forest-infested era classed as the Jurassic Period. Here, on one occasion, whilst wandering along a lonely shore, they had a singular experience, which forced home to them how utterly apart from the world around them they were.

They stood silent and transfixed. Not twenty yards away, in the swampy soil of the shore, were the footprints of some colossal, prehistoric beast. The creature itself was invisible, but its mighty imprints in the soil were quite evident—moving backwards! One after another along the shore the prints snapped into extinction, revealing where the monster was walking. After a time a group of battered trees in the foreground suddenly resumed their normal foliage, proving beyond doubt the backward passage of the creature....

The Triassic Period passed with extreme rapidity, more than thirty millions of years telescoped into months. Then a change came on the face of the world. The streaking sun and much-nearer moon became hidden by a colossal preponderance of clouds. And now an element of terror entered the minds of the youthful people at the sights they beheld—the first glimpses of a young world struggling for the existence it had gained and lost.

Storms, terrifying and overwhelming, proved the arrival of the Permian Period, the Period of clouds, upheavals and convulsions. Though these storms were always reversed they lost none of their potency. Lightning stabbed backwards, revealing the tortured landscape in an unholy glare, for miles around. A landscape of boiling, steaming lakes and writhing, lashing trees. A mighty warping of the earth's crust resulted in entire cliffs rearing up in the tempests from soil—mounds and rock piles—actually they must have been cliff-collapses of violent and terrible force.

The lakes steamed and hissed with the lightning flashes; the skies darkened to pitch-blackness. From out of the ebon vault, starting with the distant growl at the end of the thunder, and then rising up to the original awe-inspiring din, cannonaded the thunderclap itself.

Time and again the hapless four were pitched headlong from their various vantage points. Yet always they survived, to gaze again upon the horrors and destructions of a dangerously young planet.... Then, as suddenly as they came, the upheavals passed. In the eerie stillness, the streaking sun and near moon reappeared.

Backwards and backwards, through all the vicissitudes of hurtling ages, until there appeared the vividly green Carboniferous Age. Overwhelmingly excessive vegetation, festering swamps, and fetid lagoons. The accumulation of rotted vegetation was everywhere around them, vegetation that would become peat, and then through accumulating pressures and chemical change, hard black coal. Coal for the future that had already been destroyed. Paradoxes—infinite and complete....

The Carboniferous Age spun out at bewildering speed, then the luxurious rampancy of growth gave way into the gaunt Devonian Period from which it had originally sprung. Volcanic activity was again in evidence, elevating mountain ranges from the sea—but always in that strange, maddening reverse action. The Earth was becoming very, very young.

In the midst of the changing heavens the sun had become

slightly whiter in tint, indicative of increased heat. The moon had changed to a massive silver bail circling ever nearer the Earth. And somewhere four human creatures—Ann, the youngest, now only six years old, and Doctor Thurman, the eldest, now thirty-eight—watched these things and pondered what it all meant. Ann was unaware of the merciful release backward growth had given her; her mind no longer understood how terrible and catastrophic had been the history of time-reversal.

The last understandable Age of the world marched with relentless speed into the hard, primitive plains of the Devonian Period.

The Silurian Period, with its main feature of towering, gigantic rocks, was an inimical outlook. The four travelers floundered onwards, gazing up at towering, colossal cliffs of sheer rock, gray and transiently impregnable against the sky. They paused, standing on the lonely plateau to which they had come, looking out upon a scummy, slowly stirring ocean, lined along its shore with the omnipresent needle-pointed crags and buttresses...slimy, primeval vegetation sprouted along the shores.

Then—the Near-Beginning, the Cambrian Period.

Came the earliest era, the Pre-Cambrian for lack of a better name, when Earth first began to form; when it was but a primitive globe.

The skies darkened once more, and then rose up, from the midst of indescribable chaos, the most gigantic transformations. Land rose and fell visibly; deluges poured from the condensing steam of the heated lakes; clouds bulged and exploded into masses of lightning and flame, emptying their searing contents of flood and cloudburst upon a drenched and tortured world below. All in reverse, yes, but so insensate and appalling in its fury that everything merged into one common hell of a destruction and formation.

The four stood with difficulty in the midst of the terrifying light and flame, hidden from each other by steam at times—steam they were mercifully unable to touch. Ann screamed, lost

in the darkness; then her small hand came into contact with Rodney. She gripped his arm convulsively.

"The Beginning!" breathed Thurman, staring through the clouds of smoke. "See! We are going ever nearer to the Beginning!"

He spoke too soon. It was still a long way from the Beginning.

Through inestimable time, the four floundered together through a world of violently changing landscapes, crawled up rocks they could not grip, dropped into chasms of smoke and flame that did not scorch them; stood unprotected beneath the vomiting heavens.

Backwards and backwards—faster and faster. The heavens changed color, and Thurman saw that the moon had gone! It had returned to the molten Earth!

Then Thurman and Mason found themselves suddenly alone. Ann and Rodney had gone. Grief-stricken, Thurman reeled in confusion.

"Are they lost?" he yelled into the chaos.

"No," Mason whispered. "I saw what happened. It seemed for a brief instant that they had both become babies. They collapsed onto the ground, and tried to crawl towards me. Then they became huddled, lying inert. Then—then they *vanished*!"

"Vanished!" Thurman repeated dully. "You mean they have returned to nothing? Gone to whence they started?" He sat down heavily, frozen horror on his face, then suddenly he started as Mason grabbed his shoulder.

"Come on! We've got to go forward." He linked his arm in Thurman's, and together they went on.

As though it were running suddenly downhill in Time, Earth swooped with dizzying speed through the last cycles of its Time-existence....

Remaining solids changed to boiling lava; the lava to literal rivers of flame and ruin, in which mountains and hills and plains dissolved miraculously—the creations, viewed normally, of the lava itself.

Reverse! Reverse! Everything was in reverse! This knowl-

edge alone dinned through Thurman's brain as he carried onwards.

Who was this young screaming baby who crawled painfully beside him? What was he doing like this, suddenly unable to walk? He turned, suddenly unable to remember how to speak, and tried to grip Mason's hand. He stopped midway in movement, too stunned to complete the action.

Mason was sitting still, an amazing expression on his baby-face. Then his body became visibly smaller and smaller. His face shrank into a little wrinkled mass. The eyes disappeared; the whole body collapsed like a deflated bladder.

The space was empty. Joseph Mason had returned to the unknown state existing before Life.

Thurman twisted about in dumb confusion. Where was he? What was he? What was this boiling red chaos about him? This mad sense of gyrating motion? This strange and murky sky surging with bars of flaming mist?

Seemingly a nebula whirled between the flaming intermittences. Everything seemed to be on fire. Thurman's body was warping and shrinking.

There was no air! He couldn't breathe. He could not think. Something was reaching out to seize him—something blank, dark and utterly incomprehensible. It struck him, absorbed his whole being.

The endless reaches of Eternity yawned suddenly stupendous before him....

* * * * * * *

The Omnipotent Observer studied for a while the gyrating nebula from which Earth and his brother planets had been born. He tarried a little longer and watched the nebula decrease in size until it was but a speck of cosmic dust in far distant infinity. A process of countless cycles and aeons; to the Observer but a moment in Eternity.

Strange how a man had accomplished that! How that one

little Earthling had sent that one particular nebula back in time for evermore.

The Omnipotent Observer passed on his way, debating in his super-mind how far back the cosmic dust might go in Time, and, after cycles of deliberation he reached his conclusion.

Time has no end—Eternity has no beginning. The two are inseparable. Hence the dust that had once been Earth was still going backwards.... Into the Unknown, the Inconceivable—the Limitless!